THE CUPCAKE WITCH

BROOMSTICK BAKERY #1

LAURA GREENWOOD

BLURB

If there's one thing Oakley loves more than baking with magic, it's romance, even if she's never found Mr Right.

Justin wants his sister's wedding to be perfect, the only problem is that the cupcakes have magically gone wrong. Luckily, the enchanting baker behind them is willing to fix the problem.

Working together only reveals that there's something more between them, but can Justin and Oakley manage to make it work?

-

The Cupcake Witch is a paranormal romance and part of the Broomstick Bakery series. It includes witchy bakers, a wedding, and a standalone m/f romance.

ONE

OAKLEY

I TURN the sound up on the radio and start singing along to the love song blaring across the waves. There's something magical about the fact I can be listening to the same song as someone around the world, it makes me feel connected.

I pipe the buttercream onto my cupcakes and finish each one off with a rice paper flower, giving them a nice spring feel even if it's raining outside. These cupcakes are the perfect antidote to miserable weather, something I keep telling Rowen we should advertise more, but she doesn't seem to be particularly for it.

Sometimes older sisters are a drag.

Though I do wonder if she'd say the same about younger sisters. Especially as she has three whereas I only have one older sister.

The door to my workroom opens and my twin steps inside with a wide smile on her face. "You're going to *love* me," Clover says.

"Hmm?"

"Oh, are those spring vibe cupcakes?"

I resist the urge to roll my eyes. She's always so easily distracted, which is ironic when her baking speciality is the thing that takes the longest out of the four of us.

"They are," I say. "And they're for sale."

Before I can say anything else, she leans in and swipes one, taking a bite. "Mmm, you've really got the magic right on these ones."

"I know." They have just the right amount of citrus in the buttercream, mixed with a zap of magic to give it the necessary warmth. I pat my wand to thank it for its service. I don't need to do that or anything, it's just a habit I picked up from someone I went to Grimalkin Academy with.

"So good." Clover scrunches up the wrapper and tosses it in the bin.

"What did you come to tell me about?" I ask. "Or

was that just a ruse to come and steal my cakes. I don't do that with your baklava."

"Yes, you do. And do you know why Willow is selling so much more these days? She never did before."

"Clover," I chide. "Forget about our cousin for a moment. What did you want to tell me?"

"Oh, right. You have a wedding order." She waves a sheet of paper in front of me.

I reach out my hand and gesture for her to give it to me. "What are we talking?"

"There's a short turnaround, which has Rowen happy because it means we can charge them a rush fee."

"I still think that's ridiculous. I can't make fresh cupcakes until the day before an event anyway."

Clover shrugs. "It's the principle of the matter, I think."

"Well, I think it's ridiculous. I don't need a rush fee."

"You don't get all the money anyway," my twin points out. "We all take a share of the profits, remember?"

"Maybe I should change that," I mutter.

"You can try if you want. But I don't think it would work. We all benefit with the way it works. I do more hours in the shop than the three of you combined, you make more per commission but aren't as busy, Hazel and Rowen make the stuff that sells the most in the shop. It's fair and you know it."

I let out a loud exasperated sigh as if I'm not already well aware of this. We've been running our bakery the same way ever since our grandmother passed it on to us.

"I sell the most at Willow's coffee shop too."

"Hmm. True, but there are a lot fewer options there. You're not going to convince me that I should be giving up some of my share to give you more." She's half teasing, but there's also some truth in her statement.

Not that I really want to change it. I like the way we run the bakery, it makes us all equal even if Rowen is technically in charge.

"So what's the order like other than short notice?" I ask as I start loading the cupcakes into storage trays.

"The standard. They want pale colours, pearls, and a spell of newly-wed bliss."

I sigh dreamily. "That's because it's the best."

"If you say so." The expression on her face says she doesn't believe me. Which is nothing new. Clover and I have never seen eye to eye on what's romantic. It took me a while to get used to it, especially because she's my twin, but for the most part it doesn't bother me now.

"You should try some before you knock it," I say, pulling the bowl of buttercream towards me and taking out my wand.

I close my eyes and conjure the warm flutteriness of the emotion. My arm tingles and magic shoots down it, mingling with the cake topping and transforming it into something that will give the consumer a feeling like the one I just conjured. It won't last for long, but it's a feeling like no other.

I open my eyes and push the bowl towards my twin. "There are spoons over there." I point, not wanting her to dip her fingers into my buttercream.

She grabs one and sticks it into the mix so she can taste a bit. I'm not sure if she's had my newly-wed bliss buttercream before, but given the expression on her face, I'm guessing not.

"All right, that's good," Clover says after she's swallowed. "But I still prefer some of your others. Don't underestimate a good spring vibe." She switches back to the cupcake, making quick work of it. Sometimes it surprises me that my twin isn't the size of a house. Of the four of us, she's the one most likely to be eating the produce we're supposed to be selling.

"Spring vibes are good, but they're not right for weddings," I point out.

"They'll be right for mine."

I raise an eyebrow. "You've never talked about what you wanted from a wedding before."

"Because I know what you're all like. The moment I bring someone home to meet you, you'll be teasing me about the fact I want bare feet and loose hair."

"I promise I won't utter a word of it when the time comes." Maybe.

"You can mention it, but only if I tell you that I want to scare the guy off."

I let out an amused chuckle. "You've got it."

"Besides, you have enough wedding dreams for all of us, and I'm including Ash in that and he's not old enough to be thinking about getting married."

"Eighteen is plenty old enough to think seriously about romance." Especially with how serious our younger brother can be.

"Ah, so your argument is about Ash and not the fact you want a big wedding."

"I don't want a *big* wedding, I want a *traditional* wedding," I correct her.

"Is there a difference?" Clover doesn't seem convinced.

"The size of the guest list and how much it costs.

I can have a big white dress without breaking the bank, particularly if I make the cake myself."

"Won't it taste better if someone else makes it?"

I gesture to the bowl of buttercream. "You tell me."

She sighs. "You're impossible to argue with."

"Only because I've had twenty-six years of practice at it."

Clover shakes her head, but I can tell from her expression that she's amused. I know my twin well.

"Did Rowen say how big the order is?" I ask.

Clover shrugs. "It's all on the system." She waves towards the tablet sitting on my workbench. "You'll find everything on there."

"Thanks." I pick it up and swipe the screen so it opens and I can pull up the order sheet. I scan everything, marginally disappointed that there isn't anything particularly special about this request beyond the fact it involves my favourite spell. It's no matter, I'll have fun baking regardless of if there are any special requests.

"I'll leave you to it," Clover says, already heading out the door.

I turn the radio up and continue with my cakes, feeling lighter than ever.

TWO

OAKLEY

UNDRESSED CAKES SIT on every surface waiting to be covered in the light and airy buttercream I'm preparing. The only thing left to do is add a little bit of glitter to give it a good sheen, and to infuse it with the newly-wed bliss. It's a job that will take up a decent chunk of my time, but it isn't a stressful one.

I hum along with my playlist as I work, enjoying the upbeat tunes. I should probably switch to my list of romantic songs before I try to infuse the buttercream. I've done it enough times that I don't foresee it being a problem, but it's always best to be in the right frame of mind myself, it gives the magic a little bit of zing.

I stop the mixer and dip a spoon into the buttercream, checking the consistency and sheen of the frosting.

"Perfect," I say to no one in particular. None of my sisters are in the kitchen at the moment, and they probably wouldn't be able to hear me even if they were.

I lift the guard and pull out my wand. It's always better if I do this in a smaller mixer, but that's not possible when I have a wedding order to complete, especially not one this size.

With a flick of my wand, I change playlists, glad I can do things as simple as that without having to click on buttons and go through the various home screens. I don't know which witch it was who worked out how to make touchscreen technology compatible with magic, but they're a genius.

The soft croon of a romantic ballad fills the room. I close my eyes and sway back and forth, letting the feeling of bliss sweep through me. I know I don't need to do this, but I love to. It makes me feel connected to the cakes I'm making and the magic I'm performing.

One of the many reasons Rowen always refers to me as a hopeless romantic.

As soon as the feeling has overtaken all of my senses, I open my eyes and direct my wand to the big stand mixer, sending a shower of sparks towards it. The magic glitters on top of the frosting for a moment, before sinking in and mixing itself with it.

I take a clean spoon and dip it into the mix, before allowing myself a taste. The smooth texture is perfect in that regard, and the lemon flavouring is perfectly balanced, it will go well with the sweetness of the cake.

I focus on the feeling that should be welling up inside me. "Hmm. Not enough," I murmur, setting the spoon down. It just needs a little extra, but then it will be perfect.

I point my wand back at the mixer. I start the process all over again, summoning my magic and readying it to do its thing. The sparks pour forward.

"Hello, Oakley."

A thundercloud of emotion forms in me the moment I hear his voice, and the magic stops.

I turn around and glare at my ex-boyfriend. "What do you want, Craig?" I ask.

"I thought I'd come see you."

"I can see that," I mutter. "But what are you doing here?"

"I said. To come see you."

My good mood turns sour just from the way he's standing. "You can leave now."

He steps forward.

I lift my wand, not that I'll use any magic on him, which is unfortunately something he's already aware of.

"Leave, Craig." My voice shakes.

"I just want to talk." He holds up his hands.

"I have *nothing* to say to you," I say firmly, moving to put the workbench containing a copious number of cupcakes between us.

"Oakley..."

"No."

"I want you back," he says.

"And I've said no countless times. That's not going to change." I glance towards the door, hoping one of my sisters will walk in and save me from the real-life version of my recurring nightmare.

"I'll be better this time," he insists.

"You cheated on me," I remind him.

"Only twice."

"Oh, well that's okay then," I bit out. "And our definitions of twice are different."

"There were only two women."

I close my eyes and take a deep breath. "You can't say that you *only* cheated twice when they were affairs lasting for months. It's over, Craig. We are never *ever* going to happen again." Anger seethes beneath the surface, the hurt of what he did to me having faded months ago after a cleansing ritual with Clover. Now I just want him out of my life forever.

A slamming door and the creak of someone coming down the stairs cut through the tension in the room and relief crashes through me.

"Hey, Oak, have you..." Rowen starts before stopping in her tracks. "I thought I told you not to come back here," she says to Craig in a threatening tone that only a big sister can use.

"All right, I'm leaving. But I'll convince you, Oakley." The way Craig looks at me makes me certain he's going to try.

And even more certain that he's going to fail.

"Don't step foot in my bakery again," Rowen warns.

Neither of us says anything as we watch him leave. I'm simply relieved he's going of his own free will and I don't need to charm him out of the door.

My shoulders slump and I let out a shaky breath. "Thanks for saving me," I tell my sister.

"Anytime, I wish I'd known he was here sooner."

"I wish he hadn't come at all," I mutter, turning my attention back to the buttercream.

"What did he want?"

"The usual."

"Ah. He's still trying to get you to forgive him," she says, picking up a cupcake and examining it.

"I've already forgiven him. It's the wanting me to take him back bit that's a problem for me," I mutter as I dump in a healthy dose of glitter and switch the machine back on.

"Do you want to?" Rowen asks.

I let out a derisive snort that's audible even over the sound of the mixer. "Not even if he was the last man on Earth."

"Good, I never liked him anyway."

"I know. You didn't do a good job of hiding it."

"I wasn't trying to. You can do so much better than Craig."

"I can." I shut off the machine, satisfied with the way the buttercream has come out. "I promise I'm not going to go back to Craig."

"Good. Are you nearly done with the wedding order?" Rowen asks.

"It'll be ten minutes, max," I promise. "I just have to frost them."

I wave my wand at the cupcakes, making them dance around the room on a magical conveyor belt. Once they're moving at a steady pace, I turn my attention to the buttercream, lifting it from the mixer and swirling it around in the air. With a few more flicks of my wand, I have it swirling on top of each of the cupcakes.

"I'm always impressed when you do that," Rowen admits. "I can never get the magic right."

"That's because you're trying to do something too complicated," I respond as I direct the cupcakes into the trays waiting on the counter. "And you prefer to do it by hand anyway."

"So do you."

"For small batches, yes. When I have two hundred cupcakes, I'm more than happy to take a couple of shortcuts." Especially when one of the most important things to most of the brides I've worked with is that everything looks as perfect as possible.

"Good point. Let me know when you're done and I'll help you clean up."

"Thanks, Rowen. And for scaring Craig off. I appreciate it."

"What are sisters for?"

"If you're to be believed, they're for embarrassing one another and making sure that mistakes are never forgotten," I quip.

Rowen chuckles. "I'm not wrong. But they're also for protecting one another. And that's something I'm always going to do."

I smile at her, glad to have family like her.

I turn my attention back to the cupcakes, my mind already cleared of the storm Craig brought with him. I have no idea why he's back in town, but I have every intention of making sure I stay as far away from him as possible.

And failing that, I just have to make him realise that I'm never going to date him ever again.

THREE

JUSTIN

Sylvie paces back and forth, her hair done up in a contraption I'm not sure I fully understand.

"Aren't you supposed to enjoy the day before your wedding?" I ask my sister.

She turns and glares at me. "And how many times have you been married, Justin?"

"All right, I was just trying to help." I hold up my hands, but I know it's already too late and the damage is done.

She lets out a loud sigh and flops onto the sofa opposite me. "There's just so much still to do," she says. "I have to steam my dress, make sure the florist delivers to the right address after the change of venue, pick up the cakes…"

"Make sure Celia gets down the aisle too," I say.

"Are you serious right now? Eurgh, this is why I should have had a maid of honour. I thought it would be cute if I had a best man, but I was wrong, wasn't I?"

I chuckle. "On the other hand, you already seem less stressed," I point out. "And Celia is crazy about you. She'll make it down the aisle."

"She'd better. And if she doesn't, I'm blaming you," Sylvie crosses her arms as she continues to glare.

"I only understood half the words you said, but I can go and pick up the cakes, if you think that'll help?"

Her face lights up. "Are you sure?"

"I wouldn't offer if I wasn't," I point out. "And it may surprise you to know that I want the wedding to go well. I want you to be happy, Sylvie."

She nods. "I know you do. And picking up the cakes would be a real help, there's going to be a lot of them."

"Aren't you supposed to want a big elaborate centrepiece? How do lots of cakes fit into that?" The moment I've said the words, I regret them. It isn't that I'm uninterested, it's just that I don't get half the things she says when she talks about the wedding.

The only thing I really know is that Sylvie has been talking about this since we were kids and I don't want anything to go wrong for her.

She pulls out her wand and flicks it towards the wedding binder sitting on the dining room table. It bobs through the air and lands on her knee.

I watch with interest as she flicks through to the page about the cakes, sending an RSVP flying through the air. I take it in my hand and turn it over.

"Does something need to be done about this?" I ask. "It's for a Craig Sommers."

Sylvie sighs. "Right, yes, I forgot about that. He's some sort of distant cousin of Celia's. I'm not sure why he's even invited, but she was excited when she learned he was back in town. I think they used to spend a lot of time together when they were kids."

"Does it need to go to the caterers?"

She nods. "But they should have spares of each dish planned anyway. You know what people are like."

I let out a low chuckle. She has a point there, especially with Uncle Fred changing his mind about being lactose intolerant every three weeks. I wouldn't have thought it was something he could just decide against, but sometimes things are just easier to accept than argue against, and this is one of them.

"Right, cakes," she says, taking the RSVP card from me and handing me the binder instead. "This is what we're doing."

An extravagant display of cupcakes dominates the table display in the photo. They're all neatly prepared, with delicate flowers and glittering frosting, but I wouldn't say they're more impressive than a three-tier wedding cake.

"Is there something special about them?" I ask.

Sylvie nods eagerly. "They're from Broomstick Bakery."

"Ah, the place in town with the magical cakes?"

She nods. "They provide the cupcakes with a newly-wed bliss frosting. We tried some when we were doing the wedding cake tasting and it was divine." A dreamy expression crosses her face.

I frown. "You want everyone to feel newly-wed bliss?"

"Of course. That's what the day is all about, isn't it?"

"I suppose I never thought about it like that. Most people want their wedding day to be about just them."

"It still is," Sylvie assures me. "Have you not had anything from the bakery before?"

"No. I've never been sure how to feel about magically altering my emotions."

"Wait here." She gets to her feet and heads to the kitchen, leaving me more than a little confused.

I look back at the cupcake display. There is something impressive about the way everything comes together, even if I don't know the first thing about cakes. Or what they're supposed to look like for weddings.

Sylvie returns and offers me a cupcake. "It's from the bakery."

I take it from her, examining it closely. "It doesn't look any different to a normal cupcake."

"And you don't look any different to a human if you're not doing magic," she points out.

"Fair enough. What is this one?"

"It's a test cupcake for the newly-wed bliss," she responds. "So that's what they should taste like when you pick them up tomorrow." She gestures for me to eat it.

I eye the cupcake warily, but realise there's no way of getting around this. Slowly, I sink my teeth into it. I chew slowly, half expecting it to make me feel different straight away.

Much to my surprise, that isn't what happens. A warm glow fills me, but I'm easily able to distinguish between it and my own emotions.

And besides that, the cupcake itself is delicious.

"Good, right?" Sylvie asks.

I nod eagerly. "I see why you want these for your wedding."

"Good. So you'll go to the bakery first thing tomorrow and pick them up?" she checks.

"If that's what you want me to do, yes."

"And take them to the venue."

"I'll do that," I promise.

"And no eating them before you arrive," she says sternly.

I let out an amused chuckle. "There's no promising when they taste this good." I finish off the cupcake she gave me, hoping she didn't want to save it for herself. "They don't need magic to sell those."

"Maybe not, but it gives it something special," Sylvie says. "Anyway, I should head in for the night. I'll forward you the email confirmation so they know they can trust you with the cake."

"Would someone really try to take them?"

Sylvie flashes me an incredulous look. "It's several hundred pounds worth of cake. And it's good. People are definitely going to want to steal them."

"I'll guard them with my life." I reach out and give my sister an affectionate pat on the back. "I'll see you tomorrow." I get to my feet.

"Thanks, Justin."

I smile at her and leave her flat to head back to my own. It's hard to believe my sister's wedding day is tomorrow, but I've never seen her as happy as when she's with Celia and I can't wait to watch the two of them exchange their vows. I never thought of myself as a romantic until the past few weeks, but seeing the two of them prepare has definitely changed my perspective on a few things.

Or maybe that's just the newly-wed bliss talking.

FOUR

OAKLEY

I CLOSE the lid on the final box of cupcakes and place it on top of the others before taking a step back and admiring my handiwork. There's always something satisfying about seeing them all piled up like this with the tester cupcake set to the side. All I need now is for someone to pick them up and they'll be on their way to the wedding.

The door to the kitchens opens and Hazel pops her head around. "Your client's here," my sister says.

"Great, thanks. Will you send them in?"

She nods and disappears back into the front of the shop.

I'm not sure who they're going to send for the cakes, but it doesn't matter. I've dealt with everyone from brides to the cousin-four-times removed.

I smooth down my dress just in time for the knock on the door. I turn to face a handsome man with dark hair and a charming smile.

"I'm here to pick up the order for Sylvie," he says, his voice low and pleasant, making me think of warm sunshine on the perfect spring day.

"It's all ready for you," I say, gesturing to the boxes. "I just need you to sign the invoice. And there's a test cupcake here too." I pick up the clipboard and hand it to him.

A surprised expression crosses his face. "Aren't we supposed to do introductions first?"

"Oh, right. Sorry, I'm Oakley Parkes, I make the cupcakes around here." I hold out my hand.

He takes it and gives it a shake. "I'm Justin, best man at the wedding."

"Huh, you must be the first best man I've had pick up cakes." And here I am thinking I've seen everyone.

"Who normally comes?" he asks.

"Maids of Honour usually, though I get a lot of mothers-of-the-bride, I prefer the former."

He chuckles. "I can imagine, I know what my mum's been like for the last few months."

"Oh, it's your brother getting married?"

"Sister," he corrects.

My eyes widen in horror. "I'm so sorry, I shouldn't have assumed."

"It's okay, I did introduce myself as the best man when really I should have said maid of honour."

"Well, as good as I think you'd look in a peach puffy dress, I think you'd be much more dashing in a suit," I say without thinking about it.

"Ah, I'm glad you said as much, I've been debating which to wear." He grins, his amusement showing on his face. "But I don't really think I have the legs for a dress."

Despite knowing I shouldn't, I look him up and down. "I'd say otherwise."

"Good to know." He checks the invoice and signs the bottom of it. "What about that one?" He asks, gesturing to the lone cupcake sitting on the side.

"This one is the tester cupcake," I say. "I always make one extra so that whoever is picking them up so they can make sure the flavour is right." I take the clipboard from him and offer him the cupcake.

His fingers brush against mine as he takes it from me, sending a small shiver through me. "I just eat it?"

I nod. "It's just a cupcake."

He chuckles. "My sister made me try one yesterday, I know it's not *just* a cupcake."

"All right, it's a magical cupcake. But a cupcake all the same," I respond.

I watch intently as he peels back the case and takes a bite. I don't normally stare at people while they eat, but for some reason, I can't take my eyes off him.

For a moment, he looks as if he's enjoying it, but it doesn't last.

"I'm not sure it's supposed to taste like this," he says, putting it down on the table.

"What do you mean?"

"I'm not sure, but it tastes like, hmm, thunder?"

My eyes widen and panic sets in. "Let me try it." I grab a spoon from the pot in the middle of the table and scrape off a bit of the frosting. The cake doesn't have any magic in it, so I know that's going to be all right, which means this has to be where the problem is, even if I tasted it before.

The moment it touches my tongue, I discover exactly what he's talking about as the sensation of thunder settles through me.

The blood drains from my face as I remember what actually happened. I only tasted the buttercream before Craig arrived, I was so distracted that I didn't test it again after.

I cover my mouth with my hand. "I'm so sorry, I'm not sure what happened. But I can fix this."

"Do you know what the problem is?" Justin asks.

I grimace, unsure how much to tell him. "Yes," I say instead. "The wedding's today, right?"

He nods. "It starts in three hours."

"Ah."

"Is that not enough time? I'll admit to not having any idea how long it takes to make this many cupcakes."

I look at the boxes. "I think I could do it in five at a push." And I'm going to have to. I'm not going to ruin someone's wedding day because of my mistake.

"I think we can make that work," he says. "Can you bring the new cakes to the reception?"

I let out a sigh of relief. "Are you sure that'll be okay?"

"Look, the one thing I want more than anything is for my sister and her fiancée to have the best wedding day they can. And I'd rather they got the cakes that they ordered."

"So would I. I promise this kind of thing doesn't normally happen, I don't know how I let it slip through." I stare at the cupcake as if it's betrayed me.

To my surprise, Justin shrugs. "Mistakes happen. If you can fix it, then no one needs to know."

"I can fix it," I promise.

"In which case, I'll take the boxes and set up the

cakes, and you can bring the others there. Maybe I'll scrape the frosting off and eat the cakes later."

Despite the horrible situation I've found myself in, I manage a small laugh at the thought of him doing that. "I can make you a replacement batch of frosting to go with your cake. What emotion would you like?"

"Hmm, what do you suggest? Yesterday is the first time I've tried a magical cupcake."

"How about a little midsummer flirt?" I suggest before I can stop myself.

"That depends."

"On?"

"If I'll be eating it alone."

I raise an eyebrow. "So, no date for the wedding, then?"

"Is that your way of asking if I'm single?" he asks with a slight grin.

"You're the one who started it," I point out.

"That's fair. And for the record, if you wanted to stay around after you deliver the cakes, I wouldn't mind. If you're free, that is."

"I am."

"Then I'll see you there, Oakley." The way he smiles at me makes me think that he's not just being nice.

"I'll see you there," I respond.

I help him take the boxes to his car before returning to the kitchens to make the fastest batch of cupcakes I've ever made in my life. I can't believe I let Craig's appearance ruin the wedding cupcakes.

But luckily, I seem to have got myself a nice customer.

And one who is easy on the eyes too, maybe it'll be him I think about when I make him some midsummer flirt frosting.

FIVE

OAKLEY

I CHECK THE TIME, trying not to panic as it grows closer and closer to when I'm supposed to have the cupcakes at the wedding for.

"Come on," I mutter to the traffic lights. Why is it that when I'm in a rush, they're always red when I get to them?

It's a relief when I finally pull into the car park of the reception venue with barely five minutes to spare.

I get out of the car and hurry inside, leaving the cupcake boxes where they are until I know where I need to take them.

"Hey, Delilah," I say, recognising the receptionist from the previous weddings I've set up cakes here.

"Hey, Oakley, isn't it a bit late to be setting up?"

I grimace. "There was a mix-up at the bakery. Do you know where the best man is?"

"Ah, yes, I just saw him, let me get him for you." She leaves the desk and heads through a door to the left, letting the excited chatter of the wedding guests come through into the reception area.

Despite the stress building inside me, the happiness of the day takes over and a smile spreads over my face. I do love weddings.

The door opens again, and Delilah steps through with Justin behind her. My breathing hitches slightly as I take him in. The tux fits him well, and it's impossible for me to ignore how handsome he is.

Tall, dark hair, and an understanding personality. How can a witch resist? I hope I'm not about to learn that he has a partner himself. I know he implied he was single, but that's not always the truth of the matter.

I smooth down my dress, hoping he thinks I look okay, especially when he's dressed so nicely.

"Oakley," he says warmly. "You made it."

"Just in time," I say in response.

"No one's had a single bite yet, you're safe," he assures me.

"Great. I'll go get the cakes from the car."

"Do you want a hand?" He gestures towards the doors to the car park.

For a moment, I think about telling him no, but it'll really speed things up if he helps. "Sure, that'd be good."

"I think that's everything, Delilah," he says.

Interesting, so he knows her name. Which either means that he's been paying attention, or he knows her from outside the wedding. Either is possible.

"How did the ceremony go?" I ask as he follows me outside.

"Perfectly," he says, a smile on his face. "And emotional. Is it bad to admit that there were tears in my eyes?"

"It's your sister's wedding day, I think you're allowed to get emotional."

"Mmm, good point."

I unlock the car and open the boot where the cake boxes are all held securely in place by specially designed dividers.

"This is surprisingly low tech," Justin admits as I load his arms up with the first set of boxes.

I chuckle. "There's less chance of causing a problem with the cakes, and you know how bad that is. Which reminds me, I have a test one here for you." I pop it on the top of his boxes. "But I also made all three of my sisters try them before I left the bakery."

"You're not taking any chances."

"This is important to me." I put my boxes on the roof of the car while I shut the boot and slip the car keys into my bag. "It's my reputation as a baker, but I also just don't want to ruin someone's wedding."

"That's fair."

"So, where are we going?" I ask.

"Ah, we're sneaking in the back so no one knows that we're doing this," he says, already heading back into the venue.

"You didn't tell your sister?"

"There are some things a bride doesn't need to know on her wedding day."

"Well, I'm going to be extra grateful that I can take advantage of you wanting to keep her happy," I joke. "Though I'm not sure how I'm ever going to repay you."

"You can get me a drink after we've set the cakes up," he responds.

"Isn't it an open bar?" That's what the venue normally does.

He chuckles. "I'll let you order them."

"All right. A drink sounds good to me." Especially when it means I get to spend more time with the man who is making me feel a little fluttery inside.

He pushes open a side door by putting his back against it. "After you." He nods in the direction of the room.

"Thank you." I slip by, getting a whiff of his aftershave as I do and trying not to think about how nice it smells. Or how much it makes me want to make sure I get close to him when we're at the bar.

The table with the cakes appears in front of me, which is probably a good thing, I'm not sure we'd have managed to sneak everything across the room given the number of people in it.

"What do you need me to do?" Justin asks, hovering next to me with the boxes still in his hand.

"Eat the sample first to make sure it's good," I say. "Then start swapping out the cakes at the other end. Anything in a blue case is new and should be on the stand, anything with a yellow case should come off."

"Ah, smart. I didn't realise you'd done that."

"I almost didn't, but they still fit with the colour scheme this way, and we can tell them apart."

He pops his boxes down on the table and opens up the individual cupcake box I put his spare in.

He checks that no one is watching and swipes his finger through the buttercream.

My gaze fixates on what he's doing as he puts it in his mouth. I never normally get like this when someone is tasting something, but with Justin, it all feels a bit different.

This is probably all Craig's fault. If my ex hadn't shown up at the bakery yesterday, I'd never have been thinking about how differently Justin dealt with the situation.

I push the thoughts from my mind and focus on switching out the cupcakes. I'm definitely glad I chose to use the different colour liners, it makes it less likely that I'll accidentally leave one of the thunder cakes on the stand.

"That was good," he says. "I can't wait to taste the midsummer flirt you promised me." He flashes me a charming smile that makes me melt inside a little.

"That's in the bottom box with red cupcake liners," I tell him.

"You made enough to share, right?"

I let out a small laugh and swap out the top cupcake. "I did."

"Then we can have one along with our drink."

"Are you sure you want to spend this much time with me? I'm the one who almost messed up your sister's wedding," I point out.

"But you fixed it." He switches out a cupcake. "And it was an accident. I'm sure it's not the only thing that's almost gone wrong today."

"Hmm, true. Weddings can be quite disastrous sometimes."

"Especially when there are drunk relatives to take into account."

He lets out a small groan. "I've been trying not to think about that," he admits.

"Oh, so who do I need to watch out for?" The conversation is doing a good job at taking my mind off the stress of making such a huge mistake. I'm not sure if he's doing it on purpose, but I suppose it doesn't matter, I'm grateful for it all the same.

"Do you see the man in the truly terrible maroon jacket over by the bar?" He nods in the direction he wants me to look.

I scan the room, having no trouble locating him. "Wow, that suit belongs in the seventies," I mutter.

"The suit belongs in a fire. A magical one that renders it unfixable," Justin retorts.

An amused laugh escapes me.

"Anyway, that's Uncle Larry, he'll get drunk later and probably try and hit on Sylvie's new wife."

"Oof, that's bad. Because she's the bride, or just because?"

"Just because. He tried to hit on his brother once, that one was particularly bad." He opens the last box of new cupcakes and starts putting them out.

"Has anyone tried not letting him have alcohol?"

"Yes. But he's really good at turning water into wine," Justin admits. "Cliché, I know."

"That's probably why he does it."

"Mmm, good point. Right, all done. The only box I have left is our flirting cakes."

Oh I like the way he says *our*.

"I'm done too," I say as I swap out the last one. "Now all we need to do is get rid of the old cakes and we can grab that drink. Unless you're sick of me."

"Oh no, you're not getting out of it that easily." He looks down at the boxes of waste. "It's a shame we have to bin them."

"We could ask the staff if they want them and suggest they scrape off the frosting?" It's still a waste, but I'm confident the cake is good even if the frosting will make them feel like thunder.

"Let's do that," he says. "They're good cakes, it would be a shame to waste them." He picks up the boxes and heads in the direction that I assume will take us to the kitchens.

I follow behind, relieved that we've managed to get them all switched out before his sister noticed. Now I can relax and enjoy the good company I've found. And the atmosphere of the wedding. There really isn't anything like it.

SIX

JUSTIN

OAKLEY PUTS the box of cakes on the bar and hops up on one of the stools.

"What are you having?" she asks.

"Just a pint," I respond.

The bartender nods, remembering my drink from earlier.

"I'll have a white wine, please," Oakley adds. "I'll walk home and come back for the car in the morning."

I frown. "Is the shop close enough for that?"

"No, but only my eldest sister lives there."

Our drinks materialise in front of us, and the bartender goes to see to more of the wedding guests.

"So, cupcakes," I prompt.

"Are you asking because my baking is delicious, or because you want an excuse to flirt with me?" she asks, picking up her wine and taking a sip, though it does nothing to hide the satisfied smile playing at her lips.

"Can't both be true?"

"I suppose they can. But maybe I'd prefer it if you were flirting with me because you want to."

"Are you trying to tell me that your cupcakes will change what I want?"

She chuckles. "They won't, but I suppose they could if I used a stronger spell."

"Have you ever done that?"

"No, and I wouldn't. It's one thing to give my cupcakes a little extra feeling that doesn't change the way someone feels underneath, it's quite another to try and change someone's emotions."

"Good to know. And if that's the case, isn't eating one of your cupcakes basically a form of flirting?"

Oakley raises an eyebrow, her expression sparkling with amusement. "Fair point." She pushes the box towards me after taking one out for herself.

Slowly, she trails her finger through the frosting, keeping her gaze locked with mine as she does.

Despite knowing she's doing it deliberately, I can't tear my attention away as she pops her finger into her mouth.

I clear my throat and grab a cupcake of my own. Not that I need any help flirting with her. I'd do that without the help. But her cupcakes are too good to pass up. I take a bite, surprised to find a fresh strawberry flavour.

"I thought it went well with the midsummer flirt," she says, correctly guessing my thoughts.

"It does, I was just surprised."

She lets out a small laugh. "Then I've achieved my primary goal."

"Surprising me?"

"Well, I shouldn't lie. My primary goal was not ruining your sister's wedding," she admits.

"She's fine." I gesture over to where Sylvie is talking to some of our aunts. "And doing what she does best, making everyone late."

"It can't be that bad."

I let out a small laugh. "You don't know my sister. Or do you? She never said how she found out about your bakery."

"I don't know her," Oakley responds. "I'm guessing she saw one of the adverts that Rowen does. I won't pretend to understand any of it."

"Ah, you're not a technology person?"

"Technology is fine," she counters. "It's the advertising bit I don't understand." She takes a sip of her wine.

"That's fair."

"You never told me what you do for work," she says.

"Does it matter?"

"I suppose not, but isn't that the kind of question you're supposed to ask on a first da...while getting to know someone?"

For a moment, I consider pushing her further on the slip of the tongue, but I think better of it. But it's good to know that she's thinking of this as some kind of date. Though I very much intend on asking her on a real one.

"I work in social media marketing," I admit.

Her eyebrows shoot up. "Please tell me you're just saying that to pull my leg?"

"I'm not." I take a sip of my beer.

"Argh, I'm an idiot."

"You're really not," I promise. "I thought it was cute."

She glances away, but not before I see the small smile and slightly flushed cheeks she's hiding.

"Do you enjoy it?" Oakley asks.

"I do. Even if it's not what I set out to do."

"Oh? And what did young Justin want to do?"

"I wanted to be something cool like a curse-breaker. But the field is so competitive, I'm not sure what you need to do to even be considered."

"Break a major curse by the time you're twenty," she supplies.

"It certainly feels that way."

"Oh, I was speaking from experience."

"I thought you were a baker?" Though that is an assumption from what she's said.

"I am. But my cousin needed a curse-breaker for...well, it doesn't matter what for. The one she used is the witch who discovered how to make countercurses for unknown spells."

I let out a low whistle of appreciation. "And she did that before she was twenty?"

"Apparently. I don't know too much about it because I wasn't there, but you could go by her coffee shop and ask her about it sometime. My cousin's, I mean."

"Which one does she own?" I take another sip of beer, loving the way her whole face lights up when she talks about her family. I don't think she's aware she's even doing it.

"Cauldron Coffee, do you know it?"

I nod. "I've seen it on the square."

"They have excellent mochas. It's a good thing she lets me swap cake for coffee or I'd be broke."

I open my mouth to respond, but am cut off by a burly man with a determined expression on his face.

"Oakley, what are you doing here?" he asks.

Annoyance, followed by anger, crosses her face. "I should ask you the same question, Craig," she responds.

My mind races, trying to think where I recognise the name from.

"I have an invite," he says triumphantly.

The temptation to jump in and say Oakley is my date to the wedding is strong, but I hold off even if I think it will work. She seems perfectly capable of handling this guy, and I don't want to ruin my chances of an actual date with her by stepping on her toes.

"Good for you," she retorts. "Now if you don't mind, I'm enjoying the company of someone I want to spend time with, and would like to get back to that."

I look away, but only in order to hide my amused smile.

"Oakley..."

"What? Nothing's changed since yesterday," she says. "Except that now I know why you're back in town. Leave me alone." She stands up and crosses her arms, looking formidable despite the pink dress and the flawlessly done hair and makeup.

"I'm just trying to make things right," Craig responds.

"You can make things right by going away."

For a moment, I think he's going to argue more, but he finally seems to get the message and slinks away, muttering under his breath.

"Are you all right?" I ask her.

She sighs and sits back on her stool. She picks up her wine and takes a deep drink. "I'll be fine," she assures me once she's done.

"I'm going to guess he's the reason for the thunder cupcakes?"

Surprise flits across her face. "How did you know?"

"The look on your face matched the way I felt when I ate them," I respond. "And you said you saw him yesterday, that was a big giveaway."

"I wasn't very subtle with my information there, was I?"

"I won't tell a soul," I promise.

She lets out a loud exasperated sigh. "Craig's my ex. I didn't realise he was going to be here or I wouldn't have stayed. I don't want to risk ruining anything for the brides. Well, any more than I already have."

"I have no idea why he's here."

She frowns. "Aren't you supposed to be on top of

things like that as the best man?"

"I don't know *everyone*," I point out. "Especially those on Celia's side of the guest list. What's his surname?"

"Sommers."

I frown, recalling that from somewhere. "Craig Sommers."

She nods. "That's the one."

"Ah, I know, I saw his invitation last night. Sylvie said he was a last-minute addition when Celia learned he was back in time. They're cousins or something like that."

Oakley wrinkles her nose, making herself look very cute in the process. "Then I don't envy you now being related to him."

"Only very distantly, and I can probably avoid him for the most part," I quip.

She cracks a small smile, but it's nothing like the way she was smiling before.

"What happened between the two of you?" I ask.

"Are you sure you want to know? It's not a very happy wedding story."

I nod.

"There's not much to it. We were together for a few years and then I discovered he'd been cheating on me. He claimed he only cheated twice because it was only two women."

"Uh-oh." I can see where this is going. "I'm guessing you don't see it as twice?"

"Would you call an affair of ten months only cheating once?" she counters.

"Ten months?"

"Mmhmm. The other one was five months. But he still only counts it as twice and expects me to forgive him and race back into his arms."

"Which you haven't done."

"And never intend to. Just being in the same room as him makes my skin crawl." She visibly shudders, making me wish we knew one another well for me to put my arm around her.

"I'm sorry, I didn't realise."

"It isn't your fault," she assures me. "And I'm not about to let his appearance ruin the fun we were having. We should eat some more cupcakes." She reaches into the box and grabs one.

"I thought you said they don't alter real emotions?"

"They don't, but this is me signalling that I'd like to go back to flirting now," she says, taking a bite out of her cupcake.

I reach for the other one and do the same, more than happy to indulge her in what is becoming one of the highlights of my evening.

SEVEN

Oakley

I DANCE along to the music and wave my wand towards the line of sugar paper flowers that are waiting to go on my cupcakes.

They jump into the air and spin around me before making their way onto each of the waiting desserts. I hum to myself as each flower lowers into position, using my voice as a way of centreing myself while I cast my spell. I normally do this part by hand, but something about today needs magic, and I'm not entirely sure why.

The door to the kitchens opens and Hazel bustles in with a large tray of macaron shells. She sets them down on the work surface opposite me and starts to get them ready to fill.

"You seem in a good mood," my sister says as she snaps a net into place over her bright blue hair. I'm not sure why she chose the colour, but I have to admit it suits her.

"Am I not allowed to be?" I ask, finishing my task with a flourish of my wand.

"Of course."

"But?"

"I don't know, something seems different about you." She heads over to the sink and washes her hands so she can get started.

I shrug. "Who knows? Maybe I'm just having a good day."

She narrows her eyes at me. "No, it's not that."

I shake my head in bemusement. "You're not making any sense."

"And neither are you." She fills her piping bag and picks up the first macaron shell. "Why aren't you in your workroom today?"

"I wanted the company." And the echo of Craig is still there. I should burn a cleansing candle or something like that to get rid of any leftover bad energy.

"Mmhmm."

Before she can question me further, Clover

pops her head around the door between the kitchen and the shop. It seems to be a busy day for my sisters coming and going. We just need Rowen to get back from her errand and we'll have a full bakery.

"Someone's here to see you, Oak," my twin says.

"Oh? Who?"

"A guy."

A storm begins to build within me. "Please tell me Craig isn't here again?"

She chuckles. "Not Craig. Rowen told me to kick him out if he even steps inside the building."

"Then Rowen is good for something," I mutter.

"Should I send him through?"

"Who?"

"Your visitor?"

"Erm, sure, but make sure he puts on a hair net." That should put off anyone that doesn't actually want to see me.

Hazel watches me with a curious expression on her face, but doesn't say anything.

I resist the urge to stick my tongue out at my sister and tell her to mind her own business. But barely. Sometimes, being around them all the time makes me feel like a teenager and not a twenty-six-year-old with a steady job.

Clover disappears back into the shop,

presumably to give the bad news to whoever it is that wants to see me.

A small part of me assumes they're not going to come back here, so I focus my attention on the job I'm doing and start loading the cupcakes into the trays to take out front. We've been selling more of them than ever lately, and it's important that I keep on top of orders or the whole bakery's reputation could suffer.

Or that's what I'm telling myself whenever someone asks about the abysmal state of my love life.

The creak of the door pulls my attention back to it. I look up, half expecting to find my twin coming in and telling me that my visitor has gone.

But it isn't here.

My heart skips a beat at the sight of Justin with his dark hair sticking up all over the place under a hastily added hair net.

"I'm not wearing this right, am I?" he asks.

"Not even slightly, but it'll get the job done," I respond with a smile.

Hazel looks up from where she's working with renewed interest. Of all my sisters, she's the one I trust the most not to interfere.

"So I was passing by and I realise there was

something I forgot to ask you the other night," he says.

"Oh?" I try not to get my hopes up. We had a good time together, or at least, I think we did, but that doesn't mean he wants to spend *more* with me. He could just be about to ask me to make some cupcakes for another party.

"Are you free on Thursday?" he asks.

"I am." Though his question isn't helpful in letting me guess what he wants.

His whole face lights up, giving it the same boyish charm I've seen a few times already and find very endearing. "Would you like to go on a date?"

"Yes." The word is out of my mouth before I even get a chance to think about it, but I don't care, even if I had, I'd have come to the same conclusion.

"Great, I need to get back to work, but I'll message you about it?"

I nod. "You have my number."

"I do." He hesitates as if he wants to say something else, but doesn't. "I'll see you Thursday, Oakley."

"You too, Justin," I respond, feeling slightly giddy at the thought of a proper date and not the kind-of-date-kind-of-me-fixing-the-mistake-I-made-at-his-sister's-wedding thing that we did the other day.

He waves goodbye and disappears back through the shop.

I let out a heavy sigh and go back to packing up my cupcakes.

The door creaks again, filling me with hope that he's back, though there isn't really a reason he would be.

"I feel like I missed something," Clover says, eyeing me suspiciously.

"You didn't." I pick up one of the trays of cupcakes and hand it to her. "This is for the display case."

She takes it from me without saying anything.

Hazel lets out a soft snort and puts down the macaron she's currently working on. "What you *didn't* miss was Oakley getting asked out on a date."

I cross my arms and glare at her. "It's not like that's never happened before."

"Except that it hasn't happened a lot since Craig," Clover points out.

I let out a loud sigh. "It's just a date."

"With..."

"Oh, that was Justin. He's the brother of the bride I did the cupcakes for a few days ago," I say, returning to work as if they're not grilling me.

"And here I was thinking you were the kind to go

for the best man, not the brother of the bride," Clover teases.

My cheeks flame red. "He was the best man."

Clover can barely contain her amusement, and even Hazel manages to crack a smile.

"It's just a date," I say firmly. "I barely know him."

"You realise that the point of dating is to get to know him, right?" Clover asks.

"Believe it or not, I have reached my twenties knowing what dating is," I mutter.

"You should have seen her face when he walked in, Clo," Hazel says, amusement coming through her tone. "I don't think I've seen her light up like that for anything less than a full bridal party before."

I roll my eyes. "What's wrong with liking weddings?"

"Nothing," Hazel promises. "I've just never seen you as interested in a person as you are in weddings before."

"That's not true," I mutter.

"Don't you dare use Craig as an example," Clover responds.

"I wasn't going to." But perhaps I should consider that the two of them have a point given that situation.

"Well I hope you have a good time on your date with the best man," Hazel says.

"I'm going to." I'm not sure what makes me so certain of that, but something about being with Justin feels easy and right. Maybe it's simply the excitement of learning about someone for the first time, but I don't think so.

The bell rings, announcing a customer in the shop to take Clover's attention away from me. I don't think I've ever been so grateful for a well-timed entrance.

She disappears back into the front with the tray of cupcakes in her hand, leaving me and Hazel to return to work without the subject of my love life hanging in the air.

Though I have to admit that I feel even better than I did before.

I don't care if they find it amusing that I have a date with a best man, especially when I'm certain I'm going to enjoy every minute of it.

EIGHT

Oakley

"Are you ready?" Justin asks as he pulls the car to a stop outside a village hall.

"Yes, but I'm not sure what I'm ready for," I admit. "All you told me was to wear comfortable shoes and clothes I like to dance with." We're a village over from the town we live in, so I'm not really sure what we're doing here. Despite that, I can't help but feel a little excited about our date.

"Then you're ready." He grins widely and gets out of the car, coming around to my side and opening the door for me.

I know it's not a necessary thing for him to do,

but I like it all the same, it makes me feel special. Just like it does when he holds out his arm for me to take.

"Hey Sally," he says as he leads me into the hall. "Can I get two tickets, please?"

"Sure thing, Justin," she responds as she takes the money from him. "Have fun."

"I'm sure we will."

"Where are we?" I ask.

"I grew up here," he responds. "I've been helping out with a local youth group since my academy days, so I've never lost touch with it."

"And you thought bringing me on a first date to a place where everyone knows you was a good idea?"

"I thought bringing you on a *sociable* first date was a good idea," he counters. "Have you ever been to a Cèilidh before?"

"Yes, and I love them, but I never get to go to any."

"Then I have picked the best first date ever," he responds, gesturing inside the room.

It's clearly a fundraising event that's being run by some of the locals, complete with a bar being run out of a small kitchen window, but that just makes me love it more.

"You have," I agree with Justin. "Genius choice."

He beams with pride. "We should grab a drink before the dancing begins. And I should warn you that I get really into making sure I do the dances right."

"Just water is good. I'm going to need all the hydration I can get." It's impossible to ignore the excitement in my voice. Everyone in the room can probably hear it.

Even before we've started, I can feel the wide smile on my face. I can't believe this is what he thought of for our first date, but mostly because it's even more perfect than anything I could imagine.

And it tells me a lot about him.

"Oh, look, they're about to start," Justin says, pointing to the dance floor.

"Then what are we waiting for?" I ask, reaching out and taking his hand in mine so I can pull him into position.

It isn't until we're almost there that I realise how easy the physical contact is between us, and how well his hand fits mine.

We get into position beside another couple. "We need to follow the directions, right?" I ask.

He nods just as the music starts to play.

A loud cheer goes around the room and a lively jig starts to play and the caller starts taking us through the steps. It only takes me a moment to remember them from the last time I was at an event like that and to relax into it.

Justin is grinning from ear to ear, making him seem even more boyish than before. I think I can see why he's brought me here. It's a side to him that I wouldn't have been able to see if we'd been in a restaurant.

And it means we can let go and have fun. Besides, if this is important to him, then he probably wants to see how I react to being around it too.

I spin around in time with the other people in my row, the skirt of my dress flaring out as I do. I'm glad I listened to Justin's instructions about what to wear.

The giddiness doesn't fade as the band takes a break after a few dances. I'm hot and I'm drenched in sweat, but I don't care, I'm having too much fun to worry about what Justin thinks about how I look.

Besides, he seems to be just the same.

He collapses down onto a chair beside me and lets out a loud sigh. "I'm exhausted already."

"There's still most of the night to go," I point out.

"I'm not young like I used to be."

I let out a small laugh. "You're going to be out-danced by someone three times your age," I say, nodding towards an elderly couple who haven't left the floor despite the change in music. The way they look at one another fills me with joy. There's just something beautiful about love, no matter what it looks like.

"I have to save my energy or I'll never make it to the end of the evening," he responds with a grin. "Besides, I don't see you dancing right now."

"Oh yeah?" I get to my feet and head to the dancefloor, gesturing for him to join me.

For a moment, I don't think he's going to, but then he gets to his feet with an exaggerated groan.

He takes my hand in his and twirls me under his arm. I laugh as I spin, enjoying it even if the move doesn't fit with the upbeat pop song coming over the speakers.

"I have no idea what I'm doing," he admits as he pulls me back towards him.

"That's the fun part," I point out. "And you brought me here because you hoped we'd enjoy ourselves, right?"

He nods. "And because there's no chance of any frosting going wrong here," he teases.

"That was both totally deserved, and uncalled for," I respond, keeping my tone light and playful so he knows I'm not actually upset. "And you're not going to manage to get away without any food, I'm going to be starving after all of this dancing."

"Good point, I didn't think of that. It's going to be late when we get back."

"That's fine, there's a great takeaway down the

road from me, we can pick some up on the way back," I suggest.

"Are you saying that I did a good enough job with a first date that I get to see your flat?" He raises an eyebrow.

"Just to eat."

"I didn't think otherwise," he promises.

We lapse into silence and sway back and forth, letting the music guide us. I don't think I've ever had as much fun as this on a first date before, though I suppose we have had the advantage of getting to know one another at the wedding.

Even so, I think it's a sign of very good things to come.

NINE

OAKLEY

MUSIC FLOATS out of the hall, a distant hum that only adds to the atmosphere.

"It's dark out here," I murmur.

"No one thinks about putting up lights," Justin admits and pulls out his wand.

"It's as if no one thinks about those of us who need to cool down and get some air."

He chuckles. "Or maybe they're being thoughtful for those who want a private moment?"

"There's private and there's trip risk."

He flicks his wrist and a dozen twinkling lights

appear just above us, illuminating the small garden we've come out to. "Better?"

"I'm less likely to fall on my face." But more likely to fall for him. Though I don't say that out loud. It's too early for anything like that, but the romantic in me is ready to be whisked off my feet.

"You can hold my hand if you're worried about falling?" he suggests, holding it out.

A small thrill rushes through me in response. I know what he's really doing, and it's nothing to do with stopping me from falling over.

Even so, I place my hand on his and let him lead me further into the garden. The lights he conjured follow us, dancing through the air and giving the whole place a more magical appearance.

"Would you like to sit?" he asks, gesturing to a bench.

"That would be nice."

He lets go of my hand, and I immediately feel the loss, wishing he was still holding it.

He sits on the bench, leaving enough space that I have the choice about whether I want to be close enough to touch.

I take the opportunity, and smooth out the skirt of my dress as I sit, accidentally brushing my hand against his leg.

I watch him carefully for his response, but he

seems to be doing the same to me, which makes it hard to work out what's going on between us.

"Thank you for inviting me here tonight," I say, leaning back against the bench and watching the magical lights he made.

"You're welcome. Was it the right choice?"

"Definitely," I agree. "I feel like I've actually gotten to know you."

"As opposed to if we were sat opposite each other at dinner?"

"Precisely. Then you're just answering my questions and giving me the version of my story that you want me to have."

He chuckles. "I could still be doing that."

"No. You can tell when someone's being genuine. The way you talked to everyone inside, and the way they approached you made it clear that you're being completely yourself here."

"I'm glad you're able to see that."

"Did someone not?"

He sighs. "My ex. She was always asking me to put this part of myself away and move to the city so she could be closer to her friends."

"And you didn't want to go?"

"No. But I didn't stop her either. I suggested that we found a place that was in the city for us to stay sometimes, but she said that wasn't good enough."

"I'm sorry."

"There's no need to be. I don't hate her for it or anything. I loved her a lot, but we were a bad match in what we wanted in life."

"What do you want in life?" I shake my head the moment the question is out of my mouth. "I'm sorry, don't answer that, it's too personal."

"No, it isn't." He takes a deep breath. "Or it is. But after how everything ended with Anise, I don't want to waste either of our time if we're not compatible."

"That's fair. Besides, we've kind of already done the first date questions anyway," I point out.

A smile stretches across his face. "Ah, true. We did go through a lot of them at the wedding."

"It was a lovely event."

"It was. So I guess that's question one, do you want to get married?" he asks.

"I thought we were talking about what you wanted?" I tease. "But yes, I want to get married. I love the idea of a wedding and everything about it, but it isn't good enough to just have a beautiful ceremony and some nice food, it has to be about celebrating the life I'm sharing with someone, does that make sense?"

"Completely. You want a marriage."

"I do," I agree. "But I also want the wedding with a

first dance and everyone wishing us well." I let out a wistful sigh.

"You really love weddings."

I let out a bemused chuckle. "It's better you know now if you want a second date."

"Because it's where you'd want something to lead?"

"Mostly because the next time you go to the bakery my sisters *will* say something about it."

"Ah, sisters."

"Mmhmm. I think you know them well."

"I do."

"So, what about you? Do you want to get married?"

"Yes. I'm not sure I've given it as much thought as you have, but I know I want to share my life with someone like that."

"Then I think that's an excellent sign," I respond.

"I'd say so too."

A cheer goes up from inside the building, but I'm not sure what causes it. Probably just another round of dancing.

"Do you want to be a baker for the rest of your life?" he asks.

I nod. "It's a part of me. How many people get to say that about their job and truly mean it? I love working with my sisters, and seeing how happy a good cake can make someone. There's something really special about it to me. What about you, do you want to stay in marketing?"

"I'm not sure. I've always wondered what other career I could have."

"There's plenty of time to change your job," I point out. "You could do it tomorrow if you wanted to."

"That might be a little hasty."

"It might. But you get my point."

"I do," he agrees.

"Any more questions about our compatibility?" I ask, not really wanting the conversation to end. It's nice and peaceful out here, and as fun as all of the dancing has been inside, I'm glad to have an alone moment with him.

"Just one."

"Oh?"

"Do you want to go on a second date with me?"

I give a fake gasp. "And here was me thinking you had to wait three days to ask."

"That's for the *first* date," he counters with an amused note in his voice that assures me he's correctly identified my tone.

"In which case, I think it depends."

"On?"

"It's hard to make a decision on whether I want

a second date when we haven't tested one important part of our compatibility." I raise an eyebrow.

"Are you trying to ask me to kiss you?"

"Only if you want to."

"I've wanted to all night," he admits.

"In which case, I don't know what you're waiting for."

To my surprise, Justin gets to his feet and holds out his hand.

Curious, I take it and he pulls me up to join him. "What...?"

He shrugs. "I feel like a first kiss should be done standing."

"Any particular reason?"

"No." He reaches out and puts a hand on my waist, the casual pressure making me certain that this is going to end well.

I step closer and wrap my arms around his neck, bringing us even closer together. I close the gap between us and press my lips against his. I'm not sure what it is about the situation that makes me initiate. Normally, I'm the kind of person who waits and lets the other person start things, but with Justin, it feels right.

He kisses me back, not hesitating to pull me closer and deepen it. Something clicks inside me, leaving me warm and fuzzy as if I've eaten one of my cupcakes.

It leaves no doubt in my mind that this is a good fit.

We break apart, and I look up at him with a smile on my face. "I'm going to say yes to that second date," I say.

"I'm glad." He brushes a strand of hair out of my face. "I'd have been really disappointed if you'd said no."

"I do hate to be a disappointment."

He leans in and captures me in another kiss. I lean into it, enjoying every moment and feeling excited for what's to come.

If every date with Justin is going to be like this one, then I know I'm not going to be able to stop my heart from falling for long.

TEN

OAKLEY

THIS TIME there's no mystery about what's put a smile on my face and a bounce in my step. How can I not have when I had such a wonderful night with Justin? My feet may ache a little from all the dancing, but I know it's worth it.

Besides, it's nothing a little magical pain relief can't fix, and I know just who to call for that. I pick up one of the naked cupcakes in front of me and start piping icing onto it.

The door to the kitchen creaks open and my cousin steps inside, flashing me a smile. "You said you'd trade pain relief for cupcakes?" Willow places the coffee cup next to me.

"I did. There's a box of Azíl's favourites waiting for you behind the counter."

"How do you know the cupcakes aren't for me?"

I raise an eyebrow. "I just do." I pick up the latte and take a sip. "Ah, that's the stuff." I set it down and continue to ice my cupcakes.

"Dare I ask what you were doing last night to need this much pain relief this morning?" Willow asks.

"She had a date," Rowen says as she walks in, followed by my other sisters.

Uh-oh, I may be about to be interrogated.

"So it either went really well, or really badly," Willow quips.

"What kind of dates do you and Azíl go on to need painkillers when they go well?" I ask, unable to keep the disbelief out of my voice.

She shrugs. "We normally just go try a new restaurant, you know what he's like."

Mmm, she has a point there. Azíl's favourite part of the modern world is food, and he lets us all know it. Personally, I don't have a problem with it, especially because he says such nice things about my cupcakes to me.

"I didn't think you were scheduled to bake today," Clover says, studying my cupcakes intently.

"I'm not," I admit. "But inspiration struck and sometimes it's better to lean into it. What are you all doing here anyway, shouldn't someone be guarding the shop?"

"We're not open yet," Clover points out. "We're here to start the day."

"Oh, right." Oops. Somehow I didn't think about that.

Rowen chuckles. "You're really lost in a world of your own sometimes, Oak."

"It's fun. Want to try one?" I ask my older sister, holding out a cupcake to her.

"What is it?" She takes it, eyeing it suspiciously as if it's going to do something bad to her.

"Raspberry and white chocolate," I respond.

"And the emotion?"

"First kiss."

She purses her lips, clearly unimpressed by my use of an emotion like that.

"It's not going to make you want to kiss anyone," I promise. "It'll just give you the glow of a first kiss, that's all."

"Hmm."

"I'll take one," Clover says, leaning in and

snatching two of the cupcakes from my tray and handing one to Hazel.

"Great. I need to know if the balance is right." I pass one to Willow too, glad I made a full batch and didn't just do enough for my sisters to try.

"Thanks," she says as she takes it from me.

My twin peels back the wrapper and bites into it. "Mmmm, it's good."

Hazel tries hers and raises an eyebrow, nodding appreciatively.

"Fine," Rowen mutters and joins them in eating her cupcake.

I wait as patiently as I can for their feedback.

"These are good," Hazel says. "But I feel like I'm perving on your date."

Willow lets out an amused laugh. "It does give you that glow though." She lets out a loud sigh, clearly recalling her first kiss with Azíl. She still hasn't told me how that happened. I'll get the story out of her one day.

"I don't think we can sell them," Rowen says.

"I didn't make them to sell," I point out. "I made them because sometimes, baking is the only way to process something."

"I'm confused about whether your date went well or not," Hazel admits.

"It did," I assure her.

She raises an eyebrow. "So the processing using baking?"

"Oh, I just wanted to give myself time to be sure about how I felt before I do something crazy like message him and tell him when we're going on a second one."

"You're just going to tell him without asking?" Clover checks.

"Sometimes you don't need to ask," Willow puts in.

I chuckle. "He actually asked last night."

Clover lets out a low whistle. "What did you do for that to happen?"

"We just had a good time. He took me dancing."

"Ah, now it's starting to make sense," Clover says.

"It was fun," I admit. "He took me to a Cèilidh, and we danced a lot, and talked a lot." I let out a wistful sigh.

"Now she's thinking that she wishes the night didn't end," Clover supplies.

"Maybe it didn't," Willow quips.

"I did," I say firmly. "It ended with us having some food, and then he said goodnight and went home."

"I believe you," Hazel says. "You wouldn't sound so disappointed otherwise."

"I'm not disappointed." I don't think. We had a nice night, and I didn't want to ruin it with something more before the time was right. Or that's what I'm telling myself. Whether it's actually true is another matter. Then again, if whatever this is with Justin lasts, then it won't matter if we waited a few dates anyway.

My phone chimes, pulling my attention from my thoughts. I slide it out of my pocket and find myself smiling like an idiot.

< Tomorrow night too soon? >

"She's going to be even worse than normal," Clover stage whispers to Hazel.

I roll my eyes and ignore them while I type out my reply. < Definitely not. My turn to plan? >

< Is it going to be baking? > Justin replies swiftly, leaving little doubt in my mind that he's been waiting for this as much as I have.

< It's a surprise. >

< But you'll bring more cupcakes? >

< If you want me to. >

< I would. >

"Earth to Oakley," Clover says, waving her hand in front of my face.

I sigh in exasperation. "Do you have to ruin my moment?"

"You're not having a moment, you're on your phone," she points out. "What did he say?"

"That we're going out tomorrow night."

Rowen raises an eyebrow. "You're not even going to pretend to adhere to dating rules?"

"I don't see any need to. I like him, he likes me, surely it's better for us to spend more time getting to know each other, not less?"

"It's good logic," Willow says.

Rowen shakes her head in disbelief. "You found your boyfriend in a teapot."

"I wouldn't quite put it like that," Willow responds.

"How would you put it?"

"Azíl wasn't there by choice," she mutters.

"And how did you meet him?" Rowen prompts.

A part of me wants to jump in and rescue my cousin, but I like not being the centre of the conversation.

"Fine, I met him when he came out of a teapot. But that's not *why* we're dating," Willow protests. "Just how we met."

"I think it's cute," I tell her.

"That's because you love romance," Clover points out.

"I don't care. I still think it's cute." I cross my arms, almost daring her to contradict me.

"We should go open up," Rowen interrupts, defusing the growing tension in the way only an older sister can. "The cupcakes are good, Oak. You should try the flavours with a different emotion."

"I will," I respond with a smile, knowing that's high praise from her.

And it's going to be the second reason I'll have a good day.

ELEVEN

Justin

The coffee shop door opens and I look up, pleased
to find Sylvie heading towards me with a wide smile
on her face. She waves in my direction as she heads
to the counter to order her drink.

I take a sip of my own, enjoying the rich taste of
the coffee, combined with the revitalising magic
shot inside it. Oakley is right about the quality of her
coffee.

Sylvie hurries over and sits in the seat opposite
me, setting down a steaming coffee cup. "I don't
think I've ever been here before."

"That surprises me with how much you were talking about Broomstick Bakery."

She frowns. "What do you mean?"

"The owner is the cousin of the bakers."

"How could you possibly know that?"

"The witch who delivered your cakes told me." I don't add that Oakley and I got talking because there was a mistake with the order. There are some things that the bride never needs to know. The near-cake disaster is one of them.

She gives me a funny look.

"How was the mini-moon?" I ask.

"Don't think I can't tell when you're changing the subject," she mutters.

"I didn't say I wasn't." I grin widely at her, hoping she'll let it slide and not ask me too many questions about Oakley. Not that I want it to be a secret, I just don't want Sylvie to scrutinise anything too closely.

"It was good," she says, answering my question despite her slight chiding. "Though I wish it had been ten days longer."

"You could have gone for that long."

"Celia couldn't get it off work. What's the point in being a witch if you can't stop time?" she moans.

"Aren't you supposed to be happy that you get to spend the rest of your life with Celia?"

"And I am. But how many times are we going to

be able to go on a holiday that's *just* for us and no one else?"

"You can do that any time you want."

"So long as our schedules line up, and you know how hard that is."

"Mmm." She's been complaining about it for as long as they've been together. Even the man on the moon knows about her and Celia's schedule problems.

"Anyway, you were telling me about the baker?"

"I wasn't."

"And now you're going to," she says firmly. "Spill." She takes a long drink from her coffee.

I let out a loud sigh. "She forgot to give me part of the display, so came to drop it off at the wedding, and after that, we got talking."

"*Please* tell me you didn't hook up with the person who made my wedding cakes?" Sylvie demands.

"I didn't." *Yet.* Though I'm not sure if it counts as hooking up when I intend for it to be more serious than that. "But we did go on a date."

"Justin!"

"What? She's smart, cute, and knows how to make delicious cupcakes. What isn't to like?"

She rolls her eyes. "I hope you know what you're doing. After last time..."

"I'm not going to make the same mistake again."

Especially because Oakley and I have already had a conversation about it.

Before I can tell Sylvie just that, the door to the coffee shop opens and the subject of our conversation starts to enter with a large box of cakes in her hand. She struggles with the door, her face twisting in concentration.

I jump to my feet and hurry over, leaving Sylvie to stare after me as I push the door open and hold it for her.

"Thanks...hey, Justin." Her whole face lights up when she realises it's me.

"Want a hand?" I ask.

"If you don't mind?"

I take the top box from her and take it over to the counter, presuming that's where she's going with them. Oakley follows behind, smiling at the guy behind the counter.

"Hey, Azíl."

"Morning, Oakley," he responds with an indiscernible accent. "Thank you for my cupcakes."

She chuckles. "I knew it." Amusement dances in her tone, but I don't know what it's about. "There are fresh cupcakes in this one, and some cinnamon swirls from Hazel here. Willow said you wanted them?"

He nods. "We have sold out." He gestures to the almost empty display case.

"Then I'm just in time."

"I will make you your coffee."

"Thanks." She turns to me and smiles. "And thank you."

"You're welcome," I respond.

"I didn't realise you'd be here." She leans in and brushes her hand against my arm, filling the air with something undistinguishable that makes me want to reach out and kiss her, but I know we're not quite at the place where we can casually kiss hello.

Hopefully soon.

"Sylvie asked me to meet for a coffee, and I remembered that you said your cousin's was good, so suggested here. Did you know she's never been?"

"You'd never been either," she points out.

"That's fair. Do you want to meet her?"

Indecision wars on Oakley's face, but she nods. "You've met my family, I should meet yours."

"Except for your cousin."

"Mmm, true. I don't know where Willow is, but you met her other half." She gestures to the counter where Azíl is still making her coffee.

I draw her over to where Sylvie is sitting with a nosey expression on her face as if she's been trying to overhear us but couldn't quite.

"This is Oakley," I say, placing a hand on the small of her back. Oakley leans closer to me, reassuring me that she does want to do this. "And this is my sister, Sylvie."

"It's nice to meet you," Oakley says brightly, holding out her hand to Sylvie. "And congratulations on your wedding. It was a lovely event."

"Thank you. Everyone was talking about how good the cupcakes were." Sylvie shakes her hand firmly.

"Is it bad if I say I'm not surprised?" Oakley quips.

Sylvie chuckles. "I like your confidence."

"I don't have long, I need to get back to the bakery to finish an order, but it was nice to meet you." She turns and places a soft hand on my chest. "Are we still on for tomorrow?"

"Absolutely."

"Good." She pauses for a moment, looking as if she wants to lean up and kiss me, but thinks differently of it.

"I'll see you tomorrow," I say.

"Tomorrow," she repeats with another smile. She leaves reluctantly, heading towards the counter where a coffee is sitting waiting for her.

I sit back down opposite my sister, realising that there's going to be an even bigger grilling coming for me.

"When's the wedding?" Sylvie asks with a grin.

"We're going on our second date tomorrow, it's a bit early to be thinking about that," I mutter.

She raises an eyebrow. "You should tell that to the way you're acting around her."

"Aren't you supposed to be happy that I've found someone I like?"

"I am happy about that," she assures me. "I didn't realise you were heading straight to serious though."

I let out a loud sigh. "I guess I wasn't really planning on it, but sometimes you just click with someone. That's what you told me when you met Celia," I remind her.

"Don't use my own logic against me."

"I'm your brother, it's what I'm meant to do," I point out. "And it's good logic."

"Hmm, I may have to give you that one."

"Excellent, I will remember that next time you try to argue with me." Satisfaction fills me, even if it means admitting how strongly I feel about Oakley. Something about her has just gotten under my skin in a way no one ever has before, and I don't have an explanation for it. I've never put much stock in people saying that they just *know* when they meet the person who fits them, but now I've met her, I'm starting to believe it.

"Well, I look forward to getting to know her better," Sylvie says.

"Me too." A small smile spreads over my face at how true the words are. I'm going to enjoy every moment of getting to know Oakley, and hope that it will lead us exactly where I want it to.

TWELVE

OAKLEY

I STARE at the blinking cursor on the screen, trying to make sense of what it's asking me.

"Read it to me again?" Justin asks.

"It says *to unlock me, you must first turn me over.*"

He frowns. "We've looked underneath everything in the room. Where is the clue hiding?"

"I'm not sure." I glance at the clock, relieved to see we still have ten minutes to figure out the last clue and leave the Escape Room. Maybe I should have thought things through before suggesting this as our second date, but I've been wanting to come here for ages and none of my siblings will come with me. Even Ash refused, and he loves this kind of thing.

"Okay, let's think about this logically." He taps a finger against his chin and scrunches up his face in mock concentration, making him look all the more adorable as a result.

"Ah, I see Justin Holmes is on the case," I quip.

He lets out an amused chuckle. "Somehow, I don't think Justin has the same gravitas as Sherlock."

"I don't know, you sound intelligent and important."

"That's because you invited me to an escape room so I could show off my mystery-solving skills." He sounds genuinely excited about that, reassuring me that he isn't just pretending to be having a good time, he really means it.

"Either that, or you just want to be stuck in a room with me."

"I think they throw us out if we go over the time limit."

"That's a shame, I wouldn't mind being stuck here with you," I respond.

"We can arrange that later." He turns and winks, causing me to let out a girlish giggle and feel as if I'm a teenager again.

"First we need to work out what we have to turn over to get out of here."

"Have you tried the keyboard?" he asks.

I blink a few times, then do as he says, half expecting to find the answer there only to be disappointed by the emptiness underneath.

I let out a loud sigh and set it back down. "It was a good try. Should we do the same with the monitor?"

"Or..." He steps over, coming close enough that I can smell his aftershave. It makes me want to lean in even closer. Maybe I should have thought of a date that gave me lots of excuses to get him within touching distance.

Justin leans forward and runs his fingers along the underside of the monitor. "Aha." He pulls out a small tube.

"You're a genius." I kiss his cheek, wishing I'd had the courage to do that yesterday when we were in the coffee shop. I wanted to, but I worried he'd think it was inappropriate in front of his sister when we're still so early in our relationship.

Though the fact I'm already thinking of it in terms of a relationship should tell me something about how I really feel.

I push the thought to the side.

"What does it say?" I ask Justin.

"It's a string of letters." He leans down and types them into the computer.

Denied flashes across the screen.

"It's going to be an anagram," I say. "Let me see?"

He hands me the piece of paper.

I study the letters for a moment, then let out a small groan.

"What is it?"

"The passcode is *invert*."

"Ah. So turning over was a clue too."

"I'd never have gotten it," I admit as I type out the passcode.

Congratulations, you are free to leave.

I hold my hand up to give him a high five, pleased when he returns the gesture even though it's silly.

"So, how do we celebrate? Dinner? Drinks?" he asks as he slips an arm around me, clearly hoping that I don't want to end the date already.

"Ice cream," I say decisively.

He quirks an eyebrow. "That's your celebration food of choice?"

"Of course, every good win should be celebrated with ice cream."

"I'll remember that," he promises.

We say goodbye to the staff at the Escape Room and head out into the small town we call home. It's surprisingly quiet for this time in the evening, I'd normally expect there to be a good number of people milling around.

Feeling brave, I reach out and slip my hand into Justin's. He responds instantly, closing his fingers around mine. He glances to the side and smiles, revealing how pleased he is that I've made the move.

The cool air of the ice cream shop blasts me as we step inside.

"What would you like?" Justin asks.

"Hmm, triple berry with chocolate fudge sauce and hazelnut sprinkles."

He quirks an eyebrow at me. "That's a specific order."

"I know what I want," I admit.

"It sounds good, can we have two, please?" he asks the woman behind the counter.

She nods and heads off to make our ice creams.

"Please tell me you didn't do that because you don't have a favourite flavour of your own?" I ask him.

He chuckles. "My ice cream tastes change," he admits. "And what you ordered sounds good for today."

"If only it had a little flirt in the mix," I joke.

"I can bring the flirting without any magic needed," he responds instantly.

"Is that so?" I step closer to him, bringing us almost close enough to be touching, but not quite.

"Oakley?" The last voice I want to hear breaks through the happy haze of my date.

I turn, steeling myself to find Craig standing in the doorway with an expression that makes it look as if he's been sucking on lemons.

Justin reaches out and touches the small of my back in a comforting manner. "I'm going to sort out our ice creams," he says.

I nod, not knowing what else I can do, but realising that I need to do something about my ex.

"I'm busy, Craig," I say to the man in front of me.

"I can see that." He glares in Justin's direction. "You looked cosy together." His words seethe with jealousy, which riles up the anger inside me. How *dare* he act this way when he's the reason our relationship ended in the first place.

"We're not together, Craig," I remind him further. "And we haven't been in a while. I don't want to have to keep having this same conversation with you over and over again. It's over, and stop bothering me."

He steps forward and reaches out to grab me.

"Don't even think about it," Justin says, stepping between me and Craig. Despite the ice creams in his hands, he manages to give my ex a look that would make most people think twice about what they were doing. "Leave Oakley alone."

Surprise flits across Craig's face, as if he didn't

think Justin would step in. I suppose I didn't either, but I'm grateful for it. As much as I want to be able to deal with Craig on my own, it's becoming increasingly clear that my ex isn't going to listen to me. Maybe he'll listen to someone else. It's a sad state of affairs, but if it gets me some peace, then I'm okay with it.

Craig's face pinches into an expression of distaste. "You have no idea what you're getting into," he growls at Justin.

"Let's go," I say instead of responding to him. "We have our ice cream."

Justin nods, his expression softening as he looks at me. "Here you are." He gives me one of the ice creams.

Craig glares, but doesn't move to stop us from leaving.

A small part of me hopes that's going to be the last I see of Craig, but somehow, I don't think that's going to be the case. I just hope the way he's acting doesn't put Justin off getting to know me better and ruin what we're starting to build together.

THIRTEEN

OAKLEY

THE DOORBELL CHIMES and nervous excitement fills my whole body. A small part of me was worried that Justin wouldn't want to see me again after we ran into Craig again, but he seemed eager to accept my invitation for dinner.

I hurry over and pull open the door, not wanting to keep him waiting.

He steps inside and puts an arm around me, pulling me in for a kiss. I go willingly, enjoying the first sign that this is moving beyond just dating. I'm not sure why I think that's it, but there's something about the casualness of the show of affection that goes beyond just a few dates.

"Hey," he says once he's pulled back.

"Hey," I repeat back at him, my voice coming out a little faint and raspy. "Why don't you make yourself at home? I'm just putting the finishing touches to dinner, then it'll be in the oven for a bit."

He nods. "I brought the wine you suggested."

"Thanks for getting it. I thought I had a bottle, and by the time I realised, I didn't have time to get one."

"It's fine, I passed a place on the way that serves good wine. I figured they'd have a bottle. Shall I pour us a couple of glasses, or do you want to chill it more first?"

"Was it in a fridge when you got it?" I shut the front door behind him and threw the latch.

He nods.

"Then let's just go straight to the glasses. They're in the kitchen." I gesture for him to follow me, suddenly a little nervous about him being inside my home, even if he was here to eat after our first date. Something about this one feels different.

"This smells good," he says as he steps inside.

My smile widens. "Thank you, Dad taught me how to cook."

"I'll have to thank him at some point. Wait, sorry, that sounded way too serious."

"That's okay, I liked it." My heart pounds in my chest as I realise we're heading towards a conversation that could either end things completely, or make them better than ever. "So, what are we?" I blurt.

"Witches?" The grin on his face tells me that he's just teasing and knows exactly what I mean.

I let out a small laugh, and hand him a corkscrew. "I know it's a serious question, but I guess I just want to be sure that the two of us are on the same page."

"I was trying to find a way to bring it up myself," he admits. "It's still early, but I can see this going somewhere."

"Me too." The moment the words are out of my mouth, it feels better and like the nerves have finally disappeared. "I really wanted to kiss you in the coffee shop the other day."

He chuckles and sets the wine down on the island between us. He reaches out and puts an arm around my waist, pulling me closer until my hands come to rest on his chest.

"I did too," he whispers, his breath tickling my skin. "We can make up for it."

"Starting now?"

"I'd like that." He leans down and captures my lips

with his, kissing me softly at first, and then with more meaning.

I can feel the emotions coming from him, along with the promise that this is more than just a brief flirtation and a handful of dates. This could be something special.

We break apart and stare into one another's eyes, neither of us saying a word as we both let the feelings of the moment sink in.

"I need to check on the food," I say after a moment, not wanting to ruin it the first time I cook for him. The last thing I want is to give him the impression that I'm only good at baking.

Justin nods and lets me go.

I feel his absence instantly, and find myself wishing that I didn't have stuff already in the process of cooking so I didn't have to move. But I suppose there'll be plenty of time to be in his arms later. We haven't talked about what could happen tonight, but I feel like we both know it. I've invited him to my flat, and I'm making him dinner. I don't know how the signals could possibly be clearer. Even so, I'll make sure to bring it up.

Justin pours the wine while I stir the pot on the stove.

"Here." He passes me the glass. "Is there anything you want me to do?"

I shake my head. "It's mostly done, I just want to put it in the oven." I pick up the lid and pop it on the pan, glad I chose one of the models that can go in the oven as well as the stove. Rowen hates this kind of pot, but I love it for the ease alone.

I grab my oven gloves and pull open the door, popping the pan inside. "There we go. It'll be ready in twenty minutes. I skipped a starter, but did bring my A-game for dessert."

"More cupcakes?"

"You don't think that's the only thing I'm capable of making, do you?" I pretend to be shocked, but I'm secretly glad that I get to impress him.

"I would be a fool if I believed you to be incapable of anything."

I let out a soft snort. "Now you're just trying to flatter me."

"Guilty as charged." He holds his empty hand up in mock defence.

I reach out and take it with my own, entwining our fingers and enjoying how perfectly they fit together. There's something right about the way this feels.

"I'm sorry about Craig," I say as I take a seat on my sofa. I take out my wand and flick it towards the candles lining the mantlepiece. Small flames jump up from the wicks, filling the air with the faint scent of citrus and a slightly more romantic air. I set my wand down on the side table, knowing I probably won't need it much tonight.

"That's okay. I know how tough exes can be."

I let out a loud sigh.

He reaches out and takes my hand in his, giving it a squeeze. "I'm sorry he's still causing issues for you."

"Me too. So are my sisters, they've banned him from the bakery."

"That's wise," Justin agrees. "Did he cause many problems there?"

"Only the thunder cupcakes."

He chuckles. "I can't be too mad about those."

"I think I was mad enough at myself for the both of us."

"You shouldn't be," he assures me. "And we'll be able to look back at the thunder cupcakes and smile," he points out.

"Why is that?"

"Because if Craig hadn't made you feel like that, you'd never have messed up the cupcakes, and we wouldn't have gotten a chance to get to know one another."

I let out a light laugh, amusement filling me. "Are you trying to tell me that if it wasn't for my ex, we wouldn't have been able to get together."

"Exactly."

"If he ever found that out, he'd hate it," I say.

"Then I'll make sure to thank him for it next time we run into him."

I let out an unladylike snort. "I don't know if I want to be there when you do that, or not." Though I would love to see his face when he works it out.

"I'll give you a warning," he jokes.

I start to relax, a little less stressed about the disruption Craig caused even if I still wish he hadn't.

Justin reaches out and puts an arm around me, letting me melt into him and forget all thoughts of my ex. Craig is going to be nothing more than a distant memory from this point onwards, I'm going to make certain of it.

FOURTEEN

OAKLEY

I PUT the finishing touches to my cupcakes and flick my wand in the direction of the second tray, making them float in front of me and in the direction of the shop. With every step I take, I can feel the joy of a new relationship within me. I know I don't need someone to make me complete, but I can feel the excitement and joy within every part of me, and I was going to enjoy every minute.

I push open the door with my back and step through to find my twin just finishing serving the woman on the other side of the counter.

She turns to smile at me, but doesn't break her

conversation with the customer. Clover is always the definition of professionalism when she's doing front of house. Which is a lot considering she's the one who gets that duty the most. Her baklava are amazing, but they need a lot of rest time, which makes her the perfect candidate for dealing with people.

I set the tray I'm carrying down and use my wand to direct the second one to join it so I can start unloading the cupcakes into the display case, making sure to move the older ones to the back so they're easier for Clover to grab with the tongs.

There's something easy about the way we work together, and I don't think that it's just because we're sisters. This is about sharing a common goal. I know that my sisters love baking just as much as I do, and that they want to make people happy with their food. It's the reason the bakery continues to go from strength to strength.

The customer says goodbye and leaves the two of us alone now that the most recent rush is over.

Clover lets out a loud sigh and takes a seat on the stool behind the till.

"You okay?" I ask as I place the last of the cupcakes in the display case.

"I'm fine."

I raise an eyebrow, recognising the tone she uses

when she's definitely *not* fine. "You know you can talk to me, right?"

"Promise not to tell Rowen?"

Horror fills me at her words. It's never good when anyone starts a conversation with *don't tell Rowen*. "You're not going to quit the bakery, are you?"

"What? No, of course not."

"Then what's wrong?"

"I just want something more," she admits. "I love being part of the bakery, and getting to spend my time making my baklava, but I'm always ending up in the front serving customers. I want something more."

"We can try and find a way to sell more of your baklava? That way you can spend more time in the kitchen." Even as I say it, I know my suggestion isn't a good one.

"That's not quite what I want," Clover says, a note of sadness in her voice.

"What did you have in mind?" I'm assuming that she has something from the way she's talking.

"I want to write a book," she whispers, almost as if she doesn't want me to hear the words.

"What kind of book?"

"A recipe book. One that has all kinds of things in it."

"You mean like you've been doing for the blog?"

"Kind of, but it would have more pictures and different recipes. I don't know, I haven't really thought it through beyond the basic idea."

"You should do it," I say firmly. "You'd be great at it. Look at all of the responses you get to the blog. And all of the people who tag us in their baking photos. It could be the next big thing for us all, and you'd be the one spearheading it."

"But what about Rowen? I doubt she'll be happy with me diverting my attention away from the bakery itself."

"We'll work on Rowen," I promise. "You know she likes anything that will further the business."

"Hmm, true."

"We'll convince her, Clo, promise." I reach out and give my twin's hand a reassuring squeeze.

The door to the bakery opens, making both of us spring into action, with smiles on our faces and the need to serve the customer at the forefront of our minds.

My smile falters when I recognise the face of the man just entering.

"You're not welcome here," Clover says in a stern voice.

I reach out and touch her arm. "I'll deal with this," I promise.

She looks between me and Craig with an uncertain expression on her face.

"I've got this," I assure her.

Reluctantly, she nods. "Do you want me to stay?"

"Please, escape well enough for both of us."

She lets out a small snort of amusement. "Good luck."

I give her a tight smile. I'm going to need all of the luck she can possibly give me at this point.

I wait until my sister has slipped out of the shop and headed back to do whatever jobs she can find in the kitchens, then turn to the man in front of me.

"What do you want, Craig?" I demand. "I've made it perfectly clear where I stand on our relationship. I don't want to be with you, and that's not going to change no matter how many times you show up here and ask."

"I'm not going to stop," he says firmly.

"Great. Keep showing up. Keep telling me that you want a relationship with me. The answer each and every time is going to be *no*. I don't want to be with you, it's as simple as that. You can try and convince me as much as you want, but all it really does is prove to me *why* I shouldn't be with you." Beyond the cheating. That's already a pretty solid reason from where I'm standing, but he doesn't seem to have the same thoughts on the matter.

"You're making a mistake, Oakley." There's a plea in his voice, but it doesn't quite reach his eyes, as if he's decided that getting me back is one of the most important things, but he doesn't know how to do it, or even why he wants me.

"I'm really not."

"You'll regret not saying yes to me for the rest of my life."

Without meaning to, a small laugh escapes from me. "No, Craig, I really won't. I ended things for a reason."

"I've changed."

"Even if I believed that for a second, I wouldn't for much longer than that. How can you change when you don't even realise what you did wrong?"

"You're just mad because I cheated on you twice."

I let out a groan of frustration and close my eyes. "You didn't cheat on me twice, you cheated on me *hundreds* of times."

"It was only two women."

"You realise that makes it worse, not better, right?"

"I could have been picking up women every night and taking them back to mine, but I wasn't because I love you."

"Can you hear yourself?" I demand, my exasperation coming through my voice. "If you *loved* me, then you would have respected me enough not to take any of them home. Besides, this isn't some negotiation. To me, what you did is unacceptable and I don't want to ever go back to that. Now, leave me alone, Craig. You don't have any power over me anymore."

"You're making a mistake," he says again.

"I'm not. If you don't leave now, I will file a restraining order against you. And if you break that, I'll request a magical one instead." I'm not sure how effective the legal piece of paper will be, but with a magical order, he wouldn't be able to physically come near me without activating the magic. That has to be worth something.

"If you do that, then I'll tell your new boyfriend the truth about you," he threatens.

Genuine confusion fills me. "What truth?"

Craig steps forward, making me grateful for the counter between us. "Remember when you were at the academy and you decided to use those love potions?"

Cold dread sinks through me. "Nothing ever happened," I whisper needlessly. Craig doesn't care about the results of that.

Craig lets out a bitter laugh. "Maybe not. But how do you think someone you're in a relationship with would react to the fact you've used a love potion? It would certainly make most people question whether their interest in you was genuine. No one will ever understand the way I do."

The bell rings and my gaze flits from Craig to the newcomer, making all of the blood run from my face.

Justin.

Dread fills me and at the same time as righteous anger. If he overheard Craig, then I'm going to have some explaining to do.

At the same time, Craig's attempt at blackmailing me has just disappeared for good.

"Leave, Craig."

He holds up his hands. "Fine. But think about what I said. I will tell everyone."

As if I'm going to be able to think about *anything* else. Except that I can't let this loom over me. "Not if I tell everyone first." It's a bluff, but I don't think Craig knows me well enough to be sure.

Anger crosses his features, but he doesn't say anything and storms out of the bakery.

FIFTEEN

Justin

"CAN WE TALK?" Oakley blurts out the moment her ex leaves.

"Sure?" Have I done something wrong? Maybe she doesn't like that I've just come by the bakery, but I was passing and I wanted to see her.

She lets out a relieved sigh. "Give me a moment." She disappears into the back of the bakery, presumably to get one of her sisters.

A moment later, her twin appears.

"Hey, Clover."

She does a double-take. "You can tell us apart?"

I frown. "Should I not be able to?"

She shrugs. "Most people who have only known us for a short amount of time struggle."

"You're wearing different clothes," I point out.

"You'd be surprised how often people don't notice that." She sets down the tray she's carrying. "That makes me like you."

"Thanks?"

"Not as much as Oakley does."

I let out a small chuckle. "I'd hope not."

As if summoned by being the subject of our conversation, Oakley appears from the back. "You'll be okay, right?" she asks her sister.

Clover nods.

Oakley turns to me and smiles, but it doesn't quite reach her eyes. "Do you have time?"

"I'll make time," I promise, seeing that she's clearly upset and in need of that.

"Okay." She comes out from behind the counter and dusts down her dress for flour that isn't there.

I follow, confused by what's happening and what Craig could have done to upset her as much as he has.

She doesn't stop walking until we reach a small park. She heads to an empty bench and sits down, letting out a loud sigh.

"I don't think I've ever been here before," I admit as I sit down beside her.

She gives me a tight smile. "We used to come here as kids when Grandma got tired of us all hanging around in the bakery."

"I bet you were a handful."

"You can't even imagine half of it," she responds, amusement filling her voice as she thinks of the past. "I'm sorry you had to witness that." She waves her hand vaguely back in the direction of the bakery.

"Craig? He's nothing new, he's been bothering us since the day we met."

She lets out a loud sigh. "How much did you hear?"

"Just you sending him on his way."

"Ah."

"Oakley? What is it?"

"He's been threatening to tell you that I used love potions," she blurts.

I frown. "Why?" That's such a strange thing for him to have decided to try and use against her, every witch and warlock knows that love potions don't make anyone fall in love. People just brew and take them because they like the way they make them feel, nothing more.

"Why did I use love potions?"

"No, I can guess the answer to that. I meant why was he threatening you with telling me?"

"Honestly? I don't think he understands how to use them. He thinks that it would make you wonder about how you feel about me. But I want you to know that I've never used a love potion on another person. I've given them to friends before, even to an ex, but they all knew what they were drinking," she says quickly.

I nod. "They were all the rage when I was at the academy too."

She breathes a sigh of relief. "Looking back, I can see how dumb it was for us to be making and taking them."

"We all did it," I assure her. "Or at least we did."

"And yet you were surprised by how the emotions in my cupcakes worked," she half-jokes.

"I guess it feels like different magic to me, but now you say it like that, I can see the similarities," I admit. "Why does Craig think that telling me about the love potions is good blackmail material?"

"Probably because of why I stopped doing them."

"Not because one of the ingredients is technically illegal to use in potions?"

She lets out a small laugh. "It's not illegal, you just need a licence."

"Do you have one?"

"No, but that wasn't what stopped me either." She sighs deeply. "Everyone was doing them to get buzzed. It was this feeling that made you feel on top of the world and like you were the most desirable person ever. I'm not sure how it happened, but one of the couples in our dorm discovered the effects if you take a love potion with someone and then...well, you know."

"I do. Did you try it yourself?"

She shakes her head. "Not for lack of wanting to, I just never found anyone I trusted enough to go through with it." She shrugs, clearly indicating that it isn't a huge deal to her. "But then someone made one and slipped it to someone who had no idea what they were taking."

"Oh."

"Nothing bad happened, but it was the wake-up call that I needed. It wasn't so much that I thought I'd be tempted to use it on someone who didn't know, but that if it could alter my state even a small amount, then that wasn't going to end well."

"That makes sense. So the rule about not using certain emotions in the baking..."

"It's Rowen's rule, but if she hadn't suggested it, then I would have."

"Do the others know?"

She shakes her head. "I don't think so. Clover and

I were going through our phase of wanting to be opposites, so didn't really hang out that much. She studied a lot, I partied."

"Interesting, I'd have guessed the other way around."

She lets out an amused laugh. "I can see why you'd think that, but neither of us are particularly wild these days. I miss it sometimes. Not being reckless, but the not caring."

"I know what you mean. But whenever I think back to all the nights out and the partying, I feel exhausted. I don't know how I did it," I respond.

Oakley lets out a small laugh, sounding less strained than before by far. "Same. One time, we went out for three nights in a row, and even if I try and think about it now, it's too much. I'll stick to the occasional barn dance now."

"I'm glad you said that, I want to take you to more of them."

"So you're not scared off by the fact I used love potions while I was at the academy?" She half sounds like she's joking, but also like she truly worried about what I'd think.

"Unless you're about to tell me you made one that would *actually* let you change someone's emotions, then I think we're fine," I assure her.

"I'm not sure that'd even be possible," she

responds. "I could probably make something strong enough to mask their actual feelings and make it seem like some others exist, but I've never tried, and I don't particularly want to. I think there are some mysteries that just shouldn't be unveiled, even when it comes to magic."

"Ah, so you're beautiful and wise," I say, scooting closer to Oakley so I can put my arm around her.

"And talented," she says with a grin.

"Hmm, that is true. But then again, your cupcakes didn't make me flirt with you."

"They were never supposed to," she responds, shuffling closer. "They were only meant to tell you that I *wanted* you to flirt with me."

"They worked."

She turns to face me and reaches out to cup my cheek in her hand. "Thank you."

"What for?"

"For listening, for paying attention. I'm glad I met you, Justin."

"I'm glad you feel that way, because I have no intention of going anywhere."

"Good." She leans in the rest of the way and presses her lips against mine.

I close my arms around her, losing myself in everything that is Oakley. I'm glad she feels that she can trust me, and I will do everything possible to ensure that continues. One thing that's become clear to me is that I'm not ready to lose the woman I've come to care for. And I look forward to learning each and every one of her secrets, even those that involve semi-illegal potions.

SIXTEEN

OAKLEY

I FLICK my wand towards the sign on the bakery door, changing it from *open* to *closed.*

"Is this the last box?" Justin asks as he finishes loading it into the van.

"Yes." I head over to him and go onto my toes, pressing a grateful kiss against his cheek. "You know that you don't have to help me deliver them, right?"

"And miss an opportunity to miss seeing you around a wedding? Absolutely not."

I chuckle. "Most guys would be freaked out about taking their girlfriend to a wedding venue after a couple of months together."

He shrugs. "Then they're not with the right person." He puts an arm around me and pulls me closer.

I go willingly, gazing up at him adoringly. "I'm glad you think you are."

"I do," he whispers, his gaze fixated on mine. "And I'm sure that one day, it won't just be *a* wedding venue, it'll be ours."

I raise an eyebrow. "You've thought about marrying me?"

"I love you, Oakley."

"I love you too," I respond, my heart doing several impressive flutters in response to his words.

"And one day, I will marry you. But not yet."

I let out a small laugh. "It's probably a bit early for marriage," I agree. "But how about a compromise?"

"On getting married?"

"Mmhmm."

"What did you have in mind?" he asks.

"Move in with me." The words are out before I think about them. Kind of. As much as I haven't thought through how to ask him, it isn't the first time I've thought about what it would be like if the two of us lived together. No matter how many times it happens, I just can't come to terms with the way it feels when he leaves mine.

"Are you serious?"

I nod. "It's not the same when you're not there."

"I feel the same," he murmurs.

"Is that a yes?"

"Yes, Oakley, I'll move in with you."

The adoration in his eyes fills me with as much joy as his answer does.

My eyes flutter closed as he leans in and presses his lips against mine. I melt into his kiss, not caring about the cakes that need delivering, or any of the things I have to do tomorrow. The only thing that matters right now, is Justin and the way he makes me feel.

We break apart, and I find myself grinning broadly. "All right, then, back to work." I gesture to the van.

He lets out a low chuckle, the sound making me smile even wider.

"Yes, ma'am." He holds out the keys to me.

I wrinkle my nose. "Maybe not." I take them from him and get into the driver's seat, waiting for him to join me.

"How come you didn't bring the van to my sister's wedding?" he asks.

"Maybe I didn't want you to think of me as *just* the baker," I tease as I pull out of the parking spot in front of the bakery.

"I think the dozens of cakes you brought did that for you."

"Hmm, true."

"So, why didn't you?"

"We didn't think we needed it, so Rowen booked it into the garage for its service. Nothing more exciting than that, I'm afraid."

"That is rather dull."

"Mmhmm. Would it have impressed you if I'd turned up in a fancy van?"

"A little bit."

I shake my head in bemusement. "Well, I'll make sure to turn up in it next time one of your family members gets married."

"I don't think that'll happen for a while. Unless we count Celia's family."

"They are your in-laws now."

"Even Craig."

I groan. "Why are you semi-related to my ex? That's so weird."

"Hey, it's not like I did it on purpose." Amusement dances in his voice. "Have you heard from him again?"

"You know I'd have told you if I had."

"True, but sometimes bringing things like this up is hard, and I wanted to give you an opening."

"That's fair. But no, not a peep. Apparently, my last rejection of him did the trick."

"So he isn't going to tell anyone else that you experimented with love potions in your youth?" Justin checks.

I let out a loud sigh. "I have no idea. I suppose I should be glad that it's not like he can prove anything, and it's even more unlikely that he can prove anything."

"But you're still worried about it."

"A little," I admit. "It wouldn't be a good look for the bakery if it came out. But I doubt he'll be able to get me into any real trouble."

"Hmm."

"You have a thought about it?"

"Just an idea."

"And are you going to tell me what it is or keep me wondering?" I indicate left, watching the traffic but wishing I could be paying attention to Justin.

"We've had to deal with situations like this at work, and our advice to our clients is normally that they should steer into it," he says.

"What do you mean?"

"You have the bakery blog, right?"

"Yes, Clover deals with it most of the time, she posts recipes and stuff, I think."

"So use it. Write a post about why the bakery doesn't do certain types of products and you can include a part about seeing the effect of love potions on people at the academy. You don't lie and say that you didn't do them, but you also don't draw attention to it. If you get each of your sisters to write a bit about their view on the policy too, then it doesn't just look like you're the one who wants it. And if you want another perspective, you could get Ash to write something too."

"I'm not sure Ash is interested in the way the bakery runs." My brother normally keeps to himself.

"Then you need to open your eyes, because every time I've seen him at the bakery, he's been just as enamoured by it as you do. I think he wants to be part of the business, he just hasn't told you yet."

"He should be focusing on his studies," I murmur. Though now he mentions it, Ash does come to the bakery a lot. Maybe I need to pay more attention to what he takes an interest in when he's there.

"Like you did?" he teases.

"Point taken." I take a deep breath. "I'll think about the post," I agree. "I'm not sure how I feel about it when I've kept things quiet for this long, but I see how it could work."

"That's because I'm good at my job," he points out.

"You must be." I glance at him and smile. "Thanks,

Justin. It's helpful to get a new perspective on things." And to have someone who will listen to my problems and help me process them.

I'm not sure how Rowen will respond to the possibility of writing something so potentially shock-inducing on the blog, but I think she can be convinced.

Especially if I mention that it might mean that we'll never have to deal with Craig again. Which is a good argument for me to make when the time comes to pitch the idea to my sisters. I'm sure they're all even more fed up than I am about the fact Craig seems to be having trouble leaving me alone. Though the fact he's gone back to his own life seems to have given us a reprieve of sorts.

I pull the van into the parking space outside the wedding venu and switch off the ignition. "Ready to make some cupcakes look good?"

"For you, always," he responds, already halfway out of his door.

I smile to myself, enjoying the way it feels to have someone like him by my side, and knowing that this is what the next chapter of my life is going to look like.

EPILOGUE

OAKLEY

THE BACKDOOR OPENS and Justin pops his head around it. "You ready to go, Oak?"

"Just a minute, I have a cupcake for you to try."

"I'm never going to say no to that," he responds, stepping inside and shutting the door behind him. "What kind is it?"

"I made a bit of a change to the cupcakes we had on our first-almost-date," I say, setting one down in front of him.

"I thought you weren't going to sell them?"

"The blog post you suggested caused a bit of a

stir," Hazel tells him as she carefully pipes her macaron filling. "Oakley's been asked to go to Grimalkin Academy and give a talk about the dangers of messing with emotion magic."

I roll my eyes. "That's not quite what happened. Ash said that one of his professors has been trying to teach them about this stuff and wasn't doing a good job, so he showed them our blog post and I've been asked to make some cakes so that the students can try a milder version of it to try and make their point."

"Will that work?" Justin asks, picking up the cake and inspecting it.

"Doubtful, but I'm grateful I'm being asked and not having my degree taken away from me or something," I respond.

He chuckles. "I don't think they do that."

"They might."

"So what will the cupcake do to me?"

"It should mimic what a love potion feels like, but it'll only last for a minute or so rather than a few hours," I say.

"Could you make it last hours?"

"If I wanted to," I admit. "But I don't."

"Fair enough." He takes a bite. "Mmm, it's good. Oh and there's the kick, just like I remember it."

"Ah, so you had a wild youth too," Hazel teases. "And here I was thinking Oakley was the only one."

"I suspect I was wilder than Oakley," he retorts.

"I'm not sure whether I should be offended by that," I mutter.

The two of them share an amused look at my expense.

"You shouldn't be," Rowen says as she enters. "There's nothing wrong with being boring."

"Now *that* I'm insulted by," I throw back at my older sister.

An amused smile quirks at the side of her lips. "This came for you, Hazel." She holds out a letter.

Hazel puts down her piping bag and wipes her hands on her apron so she can take it.

"What is it?" I ask, my curiosity not letting me wait for her to even open it first.

"I'm not sure," Hazel replies. "It's from my old cookery school, maybe it's a reunion or something?"

"Huh, why do we never get anything that cool from Grimalkin?" I muse, but neither my sister nor my boyfriend answer.

Hazel lets out a small shriek and drops the letter.

"What's wrong?" I ask. "Are they threatening to remove *your* qualifications?" I half-joke.

Hazel covers her mouth with her hand and shakes her head. "The opposite," she mumbles.

I exchange a confused look with Rowen.

"What does the opposite mean?" Justin asks.

"I've been asked to lead a demonstration into magical baking," she says, her eyes widening. "And I've been invited by Chef DeRossi himself."

The three of us stare blankly at her.

"Chef *DeRossi*," she stresses. "As in one of the most influential warlock bakers in the world. He's my idol. And he wants *me* to run a class."

"That's amazing, Hazel," I say, beaming with pride over my sister's success.

"I can't do it. How can I go and pretend that I'm good enough to teach at his cooking school?"

"You studied there, they must think you're good enough," I point out. "And didn't you graduate with their highest honours?"

"Well, yes. But he wasn't in charge then."

"I'm not sure I see your point. If he thinks you're good enough, then why aren't you jumping on it?" I ask.

"Because it's Chef DeRossi."

"Would it help if I ordered you to do it for the good of the bakery?" Rowen half-jokes, but I can tell from her face that she's willing to go there if she needs to. Sometimes I think it might be fun if I was the eldest.

Then I remember all of the responsibilities Rowen feels like she has to carry and I don't feel so bad about being a middle child.

"Can I see the letter?" I ask.

She hands it to me without questioning it. I quickly scan it, getting more and more excited as I do.

"Hazel, this is amazing. I know it's scary, but if you don't do this, then you're going to regret it," I say, handing the letter back. "Say yes. You've got this. And we'll all let you practise your teaching on us. I love your macarons. I've been thinking that maybe we should do some kind of macaron cupcake at some point, but that's not what we should be focusing on."

Hazel lets out a small laugh and pushes a strand of bright blue hair behind her ear. "Yes to the macaron cupcakes, we should talk about that later."

"And yes to the demonstration at the cookery school?" I say.

"Maybe."

"Would it help if we pointed out you'd probably get to meet Chef DeRossi?" Justin asks.

Hazel groans. "That moves me back towards no."

"It doesn't," I say firmly. "Do this. You'll love it."

Rowen nods. "You'll be really good at it."

"See, even Rowen thinks it'll be a good idea, that's pretty much a *definitely do*."

"All right, you've twisted my arm," Hazel agrees.

"I'd prefer to say that we persuaded you," I respond quickly. "But I'll take the win where I can."

"Good, because you're not getting any better than that."

"Noted."

"I'm going to finish my macarons now," she says, barely hiding the grin on her face as she turns to wash her hands.

"So you're giving a talk at Grimalkin, Hazel's doing a demonstration in front of her idol, what about you, Rowen?" Justin asks.

My older sister lets out a bemused laugh. "I don't plan on doing anything more spectacular than the Christmas fayre this year."

"Maybe all of that will change," I say, slipping my arm around Justin. "After all, things seem to be going well for us Parkes." And I hope it continues to do so.

Thank you for reading *The Cupcake Witch*, I hope you enjoyed it! If you want to find out what happens when Hazel goes to her old cookery school to give a talk (meeting a handsome sous chef in the process!)

then you can in *The Macaron Witch*: http://
books2read.com/themacaronwitch

You can also download a free story about Ash, the
youngest Parkes sibling for free: https://books.
authorlauragreenwood.co.uk/8d24vi0je7

Thank you for reading *The Cupcake Witch*, I hope you enjoyed it!

If you want more from the Parkes siblings, then there is more coming! Each of the sisters get their own book in the series - Hazel in *The Macaron Witch*, Rowen in *The Gingerbread Witch*, and Clover in *The Baklava Witch*. Their younger brother, Ash (currently studying at Grimalkin Academy) also has a side story in the series, *The Pastry Warlock*.

Willow (the Parkes' cousin) and Azíl have their own series, *Cauldron Coffee Shop*, which follows their adventures after Willow is sent a mysterious teapot including a cursed warlock and everything that transpires after that. The series is urban fantasy romance instead of paranormal romance, but has the same magical feel to the shop. The Parkes' siblings also make an appearance in the series too!

Or, if more magic mishaps are your thing, why not try *Potion Making For Disastrous Witches*, a paranormal romance in the *Obscure Academy* series which follows Michaela, a witch who is terrible at potion brewing but needs one to help her best friend, and discovers more than just the answers to potion brewing along the way.

If you want to keep up to date with new releases and other news, you can join my Facebook Reader Group or mailing list.

Stay safe & happy reading!

- Laura

* * *

Signed Paperback & Merchandise:

You can find signed paperbacks, hardcovers, and merchandise based on my series (including stickers, magnets, face masks, and more!) via my website: https://www.authorlauragreenwood.co.uk/p/shop.html

Series List:

* denotes a completed series

The Obscure World

A paranormal & urban fantasy world where supernaturals live out in the open alongside humans. Each series can be read on its own, but there are cameos from past characters and mentions of previous events.

Cauldron Coffee Shop - Broomstick Bakery - Obscure Academy - The Shifter Season - Ashryn Barker* - Grimalkin Academy* - City Of Blood* - Grimalkin Vampires* - Supernatural Retrieval Agency* - The Black Fan* - Sabre Woods Academy* - Scythe Grove Academy*

* * *

The Forgotten Gods World

A fantasy romance world based on Egyptian mythology.
Each series can be read on its own, but there are cameos
from past characters and mentions of previous events.

Forgotten Gods - The Queen of Gods* - Forgotten Gods:
Origins*

* * *

The Egyptian Empire

A modern fantasy world set in an alternative timeline
where the Egyptian Empire never fell.

The Apprentice Of Anubis

* * *

The Paranormal Council World

A paranormal romance & urban fantasy world where
paranormals are hidden away from the human world, and
are in search of their fated mates. Each series can be read

on its own, but there are cameos from past characters and mentions of previous events.

The Paranormal Council Series* - The Fae Queens* - Paranormal Criminal Investigations* - The Necromancer Council* - Return Of The Fae*

Other Series

Purple Oasis (with Arizona Tape) - Grimm Academy - Beyond The Curse* - Untold Tales* - The Dragon Duels* - Speed Dating With The Denizens Of The Underworld (shared world) - Seven Wardens* (with Skye MacKinnon) - Tales Of Clan Robbins (co-written with L.A. Boruff) - Firehouse Witches* (with Lacey Carter Andersen & L.A. Boruff) - Valentine Pride* (with Lainie Anderson) - Magic and Metaphysics Academy* (with Lainie Anderson)

Twin Souls Universe

A paranormal romance & urban fantasy world co-written with Arizona Tape. Each series can be read on its own, but there are cameos from past characters and mentions of previous events.

Amethyst's Wand Shop Mysteries - Twin Souls* - The Vampire Detective*

ABOUT LAURA GREENWOOD

Laura is a USA Today Bestselling Author of paranormal, fantasy, urban fantasy, and contemporary romance. When she's not writing, she drinks a lot of tea, tries to resist French macarons, and works towards a diploma in Egyptology. She lives in the UK, where most of her books are set. Laura specialises in quick reads, whether you're looking for a swoonworthy romance for the bath, or an action-packed adventure for your latest journey, you'll find the perfect match amongst her books!

FOLLOW LAURA GREENWOOD

- Website: www.authorlauragreenwood. co.uk
- Mailing List: www. authorlauragreenwood.co.uk/p/mailing-list-sign-up.html
- Facebook Group: http://facebook.com/ groups/theparanormalcouncil
- Facebook Page: http:// facebook.com/authorlauragreenwood
- Bookbub: www.bookbub.com/authors/ laura-greenwood